never fall for a dragon
MATE MOUNTAIN

LOLA GLASS

Cover by Francesca Michelon
https://www.merrybookround.com/

To one of my sisters
So they can fight over which one of them it is ;)

one

ELODIE

MY EYES WERE narrow as I watched the couple argue through the coffee shop's windows. My drink sat in front of me, but I hadn't touched it since the pair started fighting.

They both had light hair and golden skin. She was tall for a woman, with killer curves, and he was clearly some kind of supernatural. He towered over her by at least eight inches, built thick and strong in a way human men just weren't, and his arms were covered in black ink tattoos.

My friend Vi would've taken one look at the guy and told me to walk the other way.

Miranda, on the other hand, would've ogled the hell out of him.

My past experiences told me that supernatural guys were pieces of shit, and to be avoided at all costs.

But my conscience had me watching them closely. If he showed any sign of violence toward her, I would intervene, even if it would land me in the hospital.

It wouldn't be the first time a supernatural asshole put me there.

The man shoved his hand through his hair. It was shaved on the sides and long and messy on top. Something about the motion was insanely sexy... and made every hair on my body raise.

I found myself standing abruptly.

He *was* going to hurt her. There was no possible way he wouldn't. Not when he was so much bigger than her, so much stronger.

I had to intervene.

My hands shook as I strode out of the coffee shop, abandoning my drink and laptop without a thought.

I pushed the doors open, and finally heard their argument.

"You can't let them do that, August," the woman argued. "You have to fight back."

The words didn't register. Not when I was so worked up that I was shaking.

If they had, maybe I would've turned around. They didn't *sound* like the words of a woman who was about to be attacked by her supernatural lover or mate.

But the words didn't register.

And I didn't walk the other way.

"I'm the one who screwed up. Now I have to play their game," the man growled.

My footsteps grew shorter, and faster.

"You know I can protect you. Leave the thunder, and—" the woman cut herself off as I stepped up next to them, narrowing my eyes at the supernatural man.

He was even taller than my ex had been.

Bigger, too. Everywhere.

"Don't touch her," I said.

My voice only shook a little.

There was a moment of silence.

A long moment.

Long enough that I had a second to wonder if the woman had needed me to intervene at all.

"You're trying to protect me?" Her voice was surprised, but not unpleasantly so. "That's really, really sweet. Thank you. But August is my brother— he's not a threat to me."

My gaze jerked toward her, and followed her hand back to the man as she gestured to him.

They *did* look a lot alike. I hadn't put that together when I watched them in the window.

He was staring at me, his eyes just as narrowed as mine had been. While mine were a soft hazel color that usually resembled a faded brown, his were bright blue. They were striking.

Gorgeous.

The word rolled through my mind before I could stop it.

"My mistake." I started to take a step back, but the man caught my wrist before my foot found the ground again.

Where his skin touched mine, fire raced up my arm.

I shuddered.

Panic should've been rising in my throat, but all I felt was that *burn* sliding into my chest before blazing through the rest of me.

"What the hell, August? Let her go." The woman tried to pull her brother's hand off my wrist, but he didn't budge.

My eyes collided with his again—and I gasped when I saw them.

The blue was gone.

In its place, was flames.

Literal fire.

"Holy shit," I breathed.

That definitely hadn't happened with my ex.

"What is this?" the woman demanded.

She must've seen his eyes too.

"Call your mate," the man gritted out. "And Jas and Eli."

I tried to pull my hand out of his grasp, but instead of letting me go, the man stepped closer.

His hands landed on my waist, and I sucked in a breath.

Holy hell, he smelled incredible.

Like campfire and trees.

And his grip felt way better than it had any right to.

"Listen closely, Fireball," the man ground out. It didn't take much for me to put together that I was the one he was calling Fireball. "You've ignited my heat. The flames in your veins will grow hotter, urging you to seek relief, and the beast in mine will push me to soothe them. If we give in, the potential bond between us will seal permanently."

"Give in to what?"

"The lust."

Holy *shit*.

What had I just gotten myself into?

"What do you want me to do?" August's sister asked.

I still didn't know her name.

"Take us to my house," he said.

"What about Bash?"

I assumed Bash was her mate. Her mate was the only one they'd mentioned without giving a name yet.

"He'll need to stay close until Jas and Eli get here." August's voice was low, and getting more gravelly by the moment. "We need to get out of the city *now*, Brynn. There are too many male eyes."

Brynn must've been his sister's name.

My gaze jerked away from his, and I looked around. I saw one guy in the coffee shop, watching us, but that was all. He looked too human to be Brynn's mate.

"What's going on?" a new, male voice asked. He sounded much more neutral than August.

The fire in my veins was getting hotter, though, making my mind cloudy and my face flush.

"Heat," Brynn said. "Help me get them to your Hummer before someone starts recording this."

"Don't touch her." August's voice was savage, and a shiver rolled down my spine.

The flames running through me *liked* his violence.

"Don't even look at the nice little human, okay, Bash?" Brynn was trying to force herself to stay cheerful. "Let's not get in a demon and dragon fight in the middle of the city.

"Demons and dragons?" My voice rose.

Werewolves and vampires were common, as far as supernaturals went. I'd met werewolves and vampires before. I'd *dated* a vampire before.

But dragons and demons?

Not common.

Not at all.

"We can give you more information when we're not standing in front of my coffee shop with a dragon who has literal fire in his eyes," Brynn said.

She wrapped her hand around August's arm, and tugged.

He used his grip on my waist to spin me around, then walked me forward. His front didn't brush my back as we moved, but some twisted part of me wanted it to.

And at his touch, the warmth in my veins *did* fade a little.

I looked over at Brynn's mate, Bash, while August walked me forward.

My eyes widened.

He was just as big, and gorgeous, as August.

He was tall and tan, with curly dark hair, and was wearing a pair of slacks with a white button-down shirt. The sleeves were rolled up to his forearms, and the top few buttons of his shirt were undone.

A low growl rumbled in my ear. "Eyes off the demon if you want to avoid a fight, Fireball."

I jerked my gaze to the road in front of us, and almost apologized. When I realized I had nothing to apologize for, I stayed quiet.

"Where are we going?" Bash asked.

"August's new place in the forest."

New place in the *forest*.

Was I about to be murdered?

I really, really hoped not.

We made it to a gigantic Jeep that looked more like an armored vehicle than an actual car.

"This is us." Brynn was still trying to be cheerful. "Take the back seat, August."

He opened the back door, lifting me into the vehicle and setting me on the seat. I slid over to make space for him immediately, but he scooped me up and set me on his lap as soon as his ass met the leather. My back wasn't against his chest, and my backside wasn't close enough to find out whether or not his body was reacting to mine.

His arms did wrap around my middle, though.

Bash pulled out of the parking lot after August gave him an address.

Brynn looked back at us with a tight smile. "What's your name?"

She was obviously talking to me, so I answered. There didn't seem to be a point in lying, considering I'd somehow managed to waltz my way into some kind of weird... relationship?

I didn't even know what to call the situation.

"Elodie."

"Nice to meet you, Elodie. Sorry it's not under better circumstances. It really was sweet of you to have my back when August and I were fighting."

"You were fighting?" Bash flashed her a look.

"I'll explain later." She set her hand on his thigh, and he captured it in his, lacing his fingers through hers. I would've preferred it if he kept two hands on the wheel while he drove, but wasn't about to start a *demon and dragon fight*.

"How long does heat last?" I asked her, my voice quiet. The fire was still burning in my veins, though it was more of a warm discomfort than anything else at the moment.

"I have no idea," Brynn admitted. "I'm a demon, not a dragon."

I didn't know how a dragon's sister could be a demon, but I didn't know much else about dragons and demons, either.

The extent of my knowledge was that demons drank lust to survive. And dragons were shifters who could switch between their human and scaly monster forms.

Brynn looked at August. "How long does heat last?"

He was silent for too long, his arms still locked around me.

Apparently he didn't want to answer.

Great.

"You can't be secretive with the woman you've just sent into heat, August. This is not the time for being protective about dragon secrets," Brynn snapped.

August's chest rumbled unhappily. "Two weeks if you sate it to seal the bond. Four if you don't."

"*Four weeks?*" Brynn demanded. "Isn't it painful?"

"Incredibly."

It was painful?

Fantastic.

I was going to spend *four weeks* in pain.

"Will I be able to make it to my classes? I'm in my last semester at SRU." Scale Ridge University was a fairly small college, but it was well-known.

I was enrolled in the software engineering program. While I enjoyed it for the most part, I was one of just a few women in most classes. It was awkward, and I was ready to be done.

"No." August answered without hesitation. "I'll deal with the school."

"You can't just *deal* with a university," I said.

"You'd be surprised what supernatural guys can deal with, when they've lived long enough. If August can't make the university work with you, Bash and his brothers will handle it," Brynn said. I didn't know how her voice was so upbeat.

Maybe because she wasn't the one dealing with literal fire in her veins.

"I said I'll take care of it," August growled. His arms tightened again, pulling me closer to his chest.

Though the warmth faded a little with the touch, my stomach clenched when I felt his erection beneath my ass.

I fought not to show any sign that I'd noticed his desire.

"Can someone please explain to me exactly what's going to happen with the heat thing?" I asked, my voice nowhere near as cheerful as Brynn's

She looked pointedly at August.

He pulled me closer, until my back was pressed to his chest.

My body relaxed more with the contact, my discomfort fading almost completely.

"My fire ignited in your veins the first time I touched you. It'll grow hotter and more painful over the next few days, and your pain will continue to increase as it does. The heat in your body will push you to me constantly, because no one else can sate it."

"I'm going to need a clearer description of *sating it*."

"Sex, Fireball. Sex will sate it. Nothing else."

"I go by Elodie. And how will the heat effect you?"

"I think you've already realized that," he drawled.

His erection throbbed beneath my ass, just for emphasis.

My cheeks warmed, and not because of the flames. "There's got to be more to it than that."

"My mind will devolve with distance between us. Unlike some kinds of shifters, dragons are not separate from our animals. My beastly instincts will grow stronger and harder to ignore, until I've claimed your body to seal our bond."

My eyes widened more with every sentence.

He added, "I should be able to control myself, but if I can't, my brothers will keep me from doing anything you don't want me to."

"You can barely handle having Bash in the vehicle with her, and he's mated," Brynn pointed out. "Jas and Eli are single, and they look just like you."

"I'll figure it out."

"I don't want to be your test subject while you *figure it out*," I argued. "And I really don't want to get hurt when you *devolve*."

Brynn responded quickly. "Not physically hurt—he can't physically hurt you. It's not possible. He's trying to say that he doesn't want to take advantage of the situation. You'll be in pain, desperate for... him to sate it, because of the fire. You won't be yourself, and he won't be himself, and that's dangerous. Right?" she looked at August.

"Yes."

"But not physically dangerous?" I checked.

"More like sexually dangerous," she said.

I squeezed my eyes shut.

"*Not* sexually dangerous," August nearly snarled. "If it gets to that point, which it won't, your pleasure will be my priority. I'll want you out of pain more than anything else. When dragons give in to heat, it always starts with the male using his mouth and fingers on the female, which doesn't seal the bond. It just escalates from there."

Okay, I was screwed.

Quite possibly in multiple ways.

"And this all happened because you touched me?" I asked.

"No. It happened because you intervened in a private conversation, putting your scent in my nose and triggering my heat. Touching you started yours, but that was unavoidable."

Lovely.

"I thought you were going to hurt Brynn, so I was trying to protect her." I gestured to the woman in the passenger seat.

"Why do you think I'm calling you Fireball?" he countered.

I scowled. "So what happens if we make it through all four of the weeks without giving in?"

"You're free to return to your life, and you'll never see me again."

At least there was that.

I just needed to survive four weeks of theoretical pain, then I could go back to my normal life.

"What if you give in?" Brynn asked.

I didn't want to know the answer to that question. In fact, I didn't even want to discuss the *possibility* of it.

"We'll cross that road if we get there," August said. "And if we do, it'll be between me and Elodie alone."

"How many couples make it through heat without giving in?" I asked.

He was silent for a moment.

A few moments.

Way too many moments.

"Not many," he finally said.

"We're going to need a number, August," Brynn countered.

"I don't have a number. If any of my dragons have survived heat without giving in, they haven't told me. Historically, I know of one."

"And?" Brynn prodded.

"And the couple resisted heat, but fell in love in the process and ended up sealing their bond anyway," he grumbled.

Great.

Just great.

We drove the last twenty minutes in silence. I forced myself to stare at the trees and mountains around us as we gained elevation, driving further and further from the main part of Scale Ridge.

When we finally pulled up in front of August's house, my body was warmer.

And wetter.

My thighs were pressed tightly together, and I'd decided I couldn't be annoyed about his erection. It was obviously the heat's fault, because I was equally turned on.

August opened the Hummer's door, then lifted us both out. His arm remained around my waist as he set me on my feet.

Bash stepped up next to Brynn, tucking her smoothly against his side. They moved together so naturally, I had a hard time looking away from them.

"I don't want Bash's scent in your house while you're losing your mind," Brynn said. "We'll sit on the porch until Jasper and Elijah get here, as long as Elodie's okay with that."

I opened my mouth to tell her I wanted her inside with me. Before I could say anything, she added,

"But, I should probably mention, we can see the lust blazing off both of you. It's a demon thing. We can't drink your lust, because we're mated, but you should know."

I slowly closed my mouth.

I had questions.

So many questions.

But considering the uncertainty of the situation, I didn't vocalize any of them.

August answered for me. "The porch works. We'll leave the door open."

With that, he walked me to the house's entrance. It looked more like a cabin to me, but I didn't say that out loud. It was one story and mid-sized, with dark green siding and large windows. The porch that wrapped around it held my attention—it would be an incredible place to work on my computer, given its undisturbed view of the forest.

When he typed the code into an electronic door lock, he didn't try to hide it from me.

0316.

The door swung open, and I looked around the inside.

There were pretty, dark brown wood floors.

Grayish-white walls, without pictures on them.

No furniture that I could see.

Brynn remarked from behind us, "Do you even have a bed, August?"

"Yep. A mattress on the floor."

She sighed.

"I'll get someone out here to furnish it in the next hour," Bash said.

Gratitude welled in my chest, and I started to look over my shoulder before August's grip on my waist tightened. "Do you want me to kill him, Fireball?"

Brynn came to my rescue. "Oh, stop it. She's not interested in Bash. He's just being nicer than you are right now. And for the record, El, Bash isn't usually the nice one. Can I call you El?"

"Um, sure."

"Perfect. Did you have a bag at the coffee shop? I just realized you don't have a purse or anything."

I looked down at myself.

No bag.

I was still wearing the same faded jean shorts and old black tee I'd had on earlier, but I'd definitely forgotten my stuff. It was the middle of summer in Scale Ridge, so the weather was beautiful during the day, but a little cold at night.

"My backpack, yeah. My laptop and phone were on the table, too." Panic rolled through me. I'd been working on a huge project all morning. If I didn't get my computer back, I'd be screwed.

"No worries, I'll take care of it," Brynn promised. "I own that *Coffee & Toffee* location. My employees probably picked your things up when you disappeared. If they didn't, we have security cameras."

I nodded, though my worry certainly wasn't fading. "Thank you."

"Of course." She gave me a small smile before sitting down on her butt on the porch, right next to her gigantic mate.

two

ELODIE

AUGUST LED me inside and closed the door halfway, then stepped in front of me.

I sucked in a breath to prevent a more embarrassing reaction, like pressing my chest to his.

He was so tall.

And strong.

And I was still wet between my thighs.

"You live with roommates," he said in a low voice.

That... wasn't what I expected him to say.

I blinked.

He waited.

"Yes. Two of them. My best friends," I finally said. "They're sisters."

"I can smell them on your skin. I need you to shower."

I blinked again.

Was he allowed to ask me that?

It was a weird request, wasn't it?

Even though he hadn't really phrased it as a request.

"Why?" I finally asked.

"Having anyone else's scent on your skin makes me itch to mark you with mine."

Oh.

Great.

"And you would mark me with..."

"My tongue."

I shivered.

My body wasn't against the idea at all, apparently.

"A shower sounds great," I blurted.

His lips curved upward, just slightly. It was the tiniest hint of a smile, but the fire in his eyes burned brighter with it. "The master bathroom has soap and a towel."

With that, his hand landed on the small of my back, and he led me into one of the bedrooms. I let him guide me, remaining quiet as we walked together.

There was a mattress on the floor, with dark gray blankets, sheets, and pillows askew. I thought it was odd that all of them were the same color, but he didn't mention it as we walked past, so I didn't ask.

In the connected bathroom, there was a towel hanging off a hook, and one bottle of four-in-one shower gel, shampoo, and who knew what else. There was an electric razor and a toothbrush on the countertop, but nothing else.

No shower mat.

No toothbrush.

"It's very lived-in," I said, before I could reconsider my sarcasm.

He chuckled, low and rough.

The sound gave me goosebumps.

"I don't live here, Fireball. Or I didn't, at least."

"When can I go home?" I asked, and both of our amusement faded.

"In four weeks, after the fire leaves your veins."

That was a long time to live with a stranger, while dealing with heat.

A long, long time.

I leaned against the edge of the bathroom countertop, putting space between us. The warmth in my body immediately increased when he wasn't touching me, turning slowly into a slight ache that reminded me of soreness after a workout.

I hadn't worked out in months, but the feeling wasn't *entirely* foreign.

And it definitely wasn't pleasant.

"I'll have to let my friends know I'm okay. They'll report me missing if I don't show up this afternoon. I should ask them to bring my clothes, too," I said.

"Everything at your place will smell like them. It's not an option."

My forehead creased. "What do I wear, then?"

"My clothes."

I scowled. "I'm not spending a month in your clothes, August."

"Then we'll order new things."

"Can't we just wash everything?"

It was his turn to blink.

I held back a snort when I realized he was surprised by the option.

A moment passed before he agreed. "That'll probably work. I'll have to buy a washer and dryer too."

Oh.

"If you don't have the money," I began.

"Money's not an issue. If it was, my sister and her mate would insist on paying." He took a step back, and slipped his hands into the pockets of his jeans. It was a casual motion, one that made him seem more... human, I guess. "Take your shower. I'll put a set of my clothes outside the bathroom door, then make sure we'll have a washer and dryer too."

"Alright."

"Lock the door," he added. "My instincts will push me back to you. When I check on you, tell me you're fine."

"Okay."

"I'll reach out to your friends to handle the clothing, too. I—"

"Don't do that. They need to hear this from me. They'll need to see me, too, if you don't want them to call the cops."

He didn't bat an eye at the warning. "Human police don't challenge dragons."

"Lovely." I brushed a few strands of hair out of my eyes. "I'm all set. You can go."

He dipped his head, then strode out of the room.

My gaze lingered on the bubble of his ass, and my head jerked as I forced myself to stop staring at him.

We were going to *fight* the heat. Not embrace it.

I locked the door behind him, then leaned up against it and let out a long, pained breath.

My mind scrambled to catch up with everything that had happened.

It was a *lot*.

And what did I even know about dragon shifters?

I forced myself to think about it.

They could shift between their dragon and human forms.

They were known to be secretive.

And... they guarded a huge supernatural prison somewhere in the mountain range connected to Scale Ridge.

It was the only supernatural prison in the world, as far as I knew.

So yeah, it wasn't surprising that the dragons didn't report to human police. They were basically the cops of the supernatural side of our society. They probably didn't answer to *anyone*.

There was a harsh knock on the door against my back.

"Fireball?"

Guess he wasn't kidding about checking on me.

"Why isn't the water on?"

"I'm just thinking. I'm fine," I called back.

If I didn't answer, the bastard could've broken the door down, and I wasn't about to risk that.

There was a moment's pause.

I wondered what he was thinking about, or what he was considering saying.

He finally said, "Alright. Let me know if you need anything. Food. Water. Toiletries."

My lips curved upward slightly. "Do you even have food or toiletries here?"

There was another beat of silence before he finally said, "I'll get them."

I bit my lip. "Don't worry about it. I'm good."

He let out a long breath, but I heard his footsteps as he walked away afterward.

Easing myself away from the door, I finally turned the shower on and stripped my clothes off. My mind continued to replay what little I knew about dragons as I scrubbed myself with August's unscented four-in-one bodywash.

Dragons could shift forms.

They were secretive.

They guarded the supernatural prison.

And apparently, they had some kind of weird mating process called heat.

I tried to remember everything he had said about heat, too.

His fire was in my veins, and would cause me pain when I was away from him. Considering the increasing warmth and ache in my muscles, that wasn't hard to believe.

It would last two weeks if we had sex, and four weeks if we didn't. But if we had sex, that would seal the bond that had started between us.

So, no sex.

Four weeks of pain.

Yay.

We would go our separate ways after that, at least. I'd go back to my life, and August would go back to his.

He hadn't told me why the heat had started, as far as I could remember. He'd said it was my fault because I interrupted their conversation and put my scent in his nose or something. But he hadn't said *why* that triggered heat.

His mind would devolve with distance between us, too. That was... something.

He'd said that when it did, his priority would be making my pain go away. I didn't understand how or why that would happen, either.

So, I had questions to ask. Questions were manageable.

What else had he said?

Hmm...

If there was more, I couldn't remember it.

The ache in my muscles was getting seriously uncomfortable. And the heat in my veins was, too.

I turned the water temperature down a bit. It didn't really help, so I just sighed and washed the soap off my skin.

August knocked on the door again. "Fireball?"

"My name is Elodie."

He ignored my statement. "How are you feeling? Are you in pain yet?"

The question caught me off guard.

I didn't want to hear that pain was inevitable.

"Fireball?" There was an edge to his voice.

"I'm not in pain. Just a little sore. And warm."

"Alright." There was a pause again. "Make sure you wash your hair, too. I could smell your friends in your hair."

I raised my eyebrows. "Why were you smelling my hair?"

"It's unavoidable," he growled. "Just wash their scent out. Please."

"Alright. I need my shampoo and conditioner from my place after this, though. This stuff will wreck my hair. No one soap can effectively do four things like this one claims."

"Your friends can bring it when they come to make sure you're alive."

With the shower on, I didn't hear his footsteps as he walked away. But, he didn't say anything else.

I grabbed more of the unscented soap for my hair.

I probably shouldn't have been going along with his requests. I probably should've expected the worst from him and braced myself for it, after everything that had happened with my ex.

But I didn't want to fight with him.

And for absolutely no good reason, I didn't think he would hurt me.

Plus, Brynn was there. She'd made it clear that she would help me if I needed her to, no questions asked.

So I would figure it out.

I'd be okay.

Somehow.

August knocked again as I shut off the water.

"I'm still fine," I said, grabbing the single towel off its hook and wrapping it around myself. It was gigantic, so it more-than covered my average-sized self. Considering how huge August was, that wasn't a surprise.

"I have clothes for you," he said through the door.

"Thanks." I crossed the bathroom and pulled it open, sucking in a breath when I found myself face-to-face with the dragon.

His eyes moved slowly down my figure. "You keep doing that. Breathing in when you see me. Why? I can't imagine you can pick up on my scent the way a shifter would."

"No, it's not your smell. You're just..." I gestured to all of him.

"What does that mean?"

"I don't know."

His eyes narrowed. "You know."

I huffed. "You're aware that you're gigantic and ridiculously gorgeous. Supernaturals are always cocky assholes—you know exactly how you affect me, and why."

With that, I plucked the messy bundle of clothes from his hand and swung the door shut.

August caught it with a massive palm just before I could close it. "What makes you believe that?"

My face flushed. "Screw off."

I tried to shut the door again.

The bastard didn't let it budge.

Instead, he said, "Dragons don't associate with other supernaturals outside the prison. I'm in deep shit with my thunder for making an illegal deal with Bash and his brothers. What makes you think you know what to expect from me?"

"That's none of your business," I said, though I was suddenly questioning my way of thinking.

He opened the bathroom door wider. "I've never been in close contact with a human woman other than my sister for more than a few minutes, Fireball. I'm not in the habit of asking pointless questions. I asked because I didn't know."

After a long moment, August finally released the door and stepped back.

Guilt rolled through me as he shut the door behind himself, turning the lock as it closed.

I'd assumed the worst.

And maybe I shouldn't have.

He hadn't done anything to make me think he was cocky, after all. He didn't seem self-conscious, but that didn't necessarily make him full of himself. He could potentially just be confident.

And while he didn't seem very *nice*, that didn't make him an *asshole*. He hadn't done anything rude or even really wrong. Our situation seemed just as shitty for him as it was for me.

So... maybe I needed to wait until I knew a little more about him to figure out what kind of guy he was.

And I probably needed to apologize.

I dried off and pulled his clothes on.

The boxers were too big, but I got them to stay up when I rolled the waistband a few times. The basketball shorts were a lost cause. No amount of rolling made them fit. His shirt hung nearly to my knees, so I tied it in an unattractive knot at my hips, where it met the boxers.

My hair felt like straw, so a grimace pulled at my lips as I started detangling it with my fingers.

Shitty hair, along with apologies.

Not to mention the uncomfortable soreness and warmth caused by heat.

And the abduction of sorts after I tried to help some girl out in front of a coffee shop.

It was a great day.

three

AUGUST

"STOP PACING AND GET OUT HERE," Brynn called through the front door. She and Bash were still on the front porch, and off their phones for the first time in twenty minutes.

They were organizing things for me.

Furniture.

Food.

Shampoo.

All the shit my instincts screamed that I should've provided for my mate.

And I really needed to stop thinking about her as mine.

Elodie.

Her name was lyrical. It didn't fit the fire I'd seen from her.

It took more control than I ever would've imagined to keep myself from breaking into that bathroom while she was showering. Not to see her naked—though I wanted that too. Badly. Painfully badly.

But because every fiber of my being was dragging me back to her side.

The bond between a dragon shifter and his mate was a codependent one, which was why most of us avoided it like the plague.

A dragon couldn't fly without his mate. Shifting without her at his side became physically impossible. His mate, on the other hand, would go into heat every month after sealing the bond. It was a week of hell for her, month after month, if he didn't soothe it for her.

Dragon shifters were always born male, so our mountains were the safest places for us. No unmated women were allowed there, ever. When a female dragon was born, she was born human, and raised among others like her.

The rest of us stayed out of their towns and cities as much as possible to avoid being chained to a mate, never interacting with human women if we could help it.

But it was obviously too late for me.

Now, I had to survive heat.

Brynn waved me toward her, so I reluctantly made my way out. When she gestured, I sat down on the porch's wooden planks beside her.

"Jas and Eli are on their way. Apparently, they have a few other guys from the thunder with them," she said.

I ran a hand through my hair. "They'll want to make sure I've actually sent my female into heat."

"*Your* female?" She eyed me.

"*A* female," I corrected.

It felt like a lie.

Sounded like one, too.

Hell, it even irritated me a little to consider that Elodie might not be mine.

It irritated me more to know that she'd already decided I was an asshole. It was for the better—but pissed me off anyway.

"What will they do when they realize it's the truth?" Bash asked.

I shouldn't have answered.

I shouldn't have told them a damn thing about dragons, or our heat. But they were family, and I was tired of keeping things from them.

And as loyal as I was to the thunder I'd been running for three decades, I thought my sister deserved most of the truth. Some things had to be kept secret.

"They'll wait until after it's over to lock me up. If we seal the bond, they'll lock her up too."

Brynn's eyes widened. "Seriously?"

"They would have to. I'd go insane without her." Not having access to my wings, while being locked in prison?

It would be a death sentence.

The thunder wanted to punish me, but it was only six months of imprisonment. I'd make it through, if I wasn't mated.

And I sure as hell wasn't about to be the reason my mate went to jail, or spent six months surrounded by dangerous supernaturals who wanted her dead just because she was mine. She was human; she wouldn't even be able to protect herself without me.

"So you can't seal the bond." Brynn sighed. "It's too bad. I like her."

"You barely know her," I said.

"She thought she was rescuing me from you when she interrupted us, and did it even though she was clearly scared. That's all I need to know."

"If most dragons don't make it through heat without a bond, it might be best to separate yourself from her entirely," Bash suggested.

Brynn smacked him on the arm.

"I would if I could, but it's not an option. She would be in too much pain without me here. That knowledge would drive me to insanity—and the past has proven that mental change irreversible. The thunder would have to kill me afterward."

"Has anyone tried painkillers before?" Bash asked.

Brynn shot him a look. He tugged her closer, squeezing her hip lightly, and she leaned against him more.

"Many times. They're all useless against heat's magic. In the past, some dragons have paid witches to try to keep their mates out of pain, too, but it never helped."

"Well, that sucks," Brynn said.

"Yup." I closed my eyes, forcing myself to breathe through a wave of magic driving me back to the bathroom. To her side. "Did you find her bag?"

"Yeah, my manager had already grabbed it. One of my baristas is driving it over as we speak. She should be here soon. Someone recorded the whole exchange between us, and everyone in the shop was watching, but there was no sound. We should be fine. Zander's working on taking the videos down right now, just to be safe, too."

Zander was one of Bash's brothers. The three of them ran a group of demons and humans who took out vampires that hurt humans. Most vampires were decent, but some were violent. And those bastards didn't deserve to keep living.

Dragons were supposed to be neutral toward other supernaturals. We weren't supposed to take sides.

Which was one of the reasons the thunder didn't want me leading them.

I couldn't say I was broken-hearted about it. I'd only taken the leadership role when my father passed on because he asked me to. I'd given it everything I had, and it had been clear for years that I wasn't a good fit for them.

Though I originally hung on for my dad's sake, it felt like a weight off my shoulders when they finally asked my brother to take over.

Jasper would do a hell of a lot better than I had.

"Thanks. She was worried about that."

"I know. Did you ask her what she was studying?"

"No. Did you?"

"Nope." Brynn leaned her head against Bash's shoulder, studying me. "You need to get to know her over the next few weeks. If she's stuck here, in pain, being friendly is the least you can do."

"Getting to know her is a bad idea. If I let myself get attached to her, walking away will become an impossibility."

And if I couldn't walk away, I'd end up dragging her pretty little ass to prison with me.

Which I couldn't allow to happen, for many reasons.

"Bash thought that when he first met me, too," Brynn countered. "You could survive the next few weeks, and come back to find her after you get out of—"

The bathroom door opened behind us, and she cut herself off.

I couldn't stop myself from looking over my shoulder to watch her leave the bedroom.

Her black hair was a mess, falling in tangled strands around her face and over her shoulders. It was long enough to hit the middle of her back—long enough that I itched to wrap my hands in it.

My clothes nearly swallowed her whole, so she had rolled the boxers a few times, exposing most of those sexy, soft legs. She'd tied the t-shirt in a messy knot at her hip, too. I could see the points of her nipples through the thin, black fabric, and it made my cock throb painfully.

Fuck me, she was gorgeous.

And her scent...

I could already smell it in the air.

My entire body clenched as I fought the urge—the *need*—to go to her side and take her in my arms.

To taste her.

Talk to her.

Make her mine.

"Was my backpack still there?" she asked, her gaze going straight to Brynn.

I wanted her to look at me.

My sister smiled. "Yep. One of my baristas is on her way here with it right now."

Elodie's shoulders relaxed. "Thank you. I've been working on a big project and didn't want to lose everything."

"What are you studying?" Brynn's gaze flicked to me, almost... challenging me.

I ignored her challenge.

I couldn't let myself get any more attached to the woman than I already was.

"Software engineering. It could end up difficult to get a job, but I love it," she admitted.

I couldn't help but be intrigued by her admission, even if I wasn't allowed to show it.

Brynn waved her toward us, and Elodie reluctantly stepped out onto the porch. My sister shooed me away with her hands, so I scowled, but made space between Brynn and I for Elodie.

My female reluctantly sat down on the porch beside me.

It took everything I had not to wrap an arm around her back and pull her to my side.

"I know a guy who might be able to get you a job. My brother-in-law. As long as you're not against tracking down violent vampires so a group of demons can kill them," Brynn offered.

Elodie's eyes widened. "That's a thing?"

"Keep it on the down-low, but yeah."

"I'm definitely in. If he's interested in me, I guess."

I couldn't stop the growl that vibrated my chest.

"Not romantically," she added hastily. "I'm not looking for —that."

Brynn smiled. "He's happily mated, as August already knows, but I'll talk to him. Give me your phone number?"

"Of course."

Brynn finished putting it in her phone just as a tiny white car pulled up to the house. A high-school-aged girl got out just long enough to hug Brynn and give her a simple, gray backpack.

As the car drove away, Brynn handed the bag over to Elodie, who accepted it with a grateful expression.

She checked a few of the bag's pockets before pulling her phone out and looking at the screen. "I need a minute to call my friends."

Brynn squeezed her arm lightly. "Take all the time you need, El."

Elodie slipped back inside the cabin, shutting the door behind her that time.

My whole body clenched as I fought the urge to go after her.

"How hard is it to keep your distance?" Bash asked.

I ground my teeth against the need to follow her, unable to answer him.

"You're fucked," he said, after a moment of silence.

"No kidding."

It was going to be the longest four weeks of my life.

four

ELODIE

I SCROLLED through the texts I'd missed, worrying more with every one I read.

They were supposed to meet me at the coffee shop after their last class ended, so I'd known they'd be panicking when they couldn't find me. Reading the messages still made me feel bad about it, though.

VI

Where are you?

We're here

I don't see your stuff

Are you in the bathroom?

RANDA

Hello?

Elodie??

VI

I just checked the bathroom, and it's empty

Where are you?

RANDA

I just stalked your location, and it says you're here

But you're not here

So where are you?

VI

I'm calling the police if we don't hear from you soon

You're moving now. Why are you moving now?

Where the hell are you going?

RANDA

You know we have no choice but to follow you

VI

You're not with Dickwad, are you?

Dickwad was the nickname I'd given my ex. They called him that too.

VI

If he hurts you again, we're going to jail for murder

RANDA

We can share a room there too, it'll be fun

I snorted.

A quick look at the app we used to track each other's locations made me grimace.

They were only a few minutes from August's cabin.

I dialed Randa's number, knowing Viola would be driving. Randa was the slowest driver known to man, and it irritated Vi to no end.

"What the hell is going on?" Vi demanded, when Randa answered. I knew I was on speaker; they always put me on speaker when they were together. I did the same when I was with one of them, too.

"It's a long story." I squeezed my eyes shut.

The ache in my body had gotten worse when I got out of the shower. The warmth had, too.

Even more frustratingly, I'd had a hard time not scooting closer to August on the porch. Some insane part of me desperately wanted to touch him.

And apologize to him.

"Tell me it doesn't involve Dickwad," Randa said.

"It doesn't. It does involve supernaturals, though."

"What kind of supernaturals?"

"Demons and dragons. Mostly, dragons."

"How did you get involved with *dragons*?" Vi asked, her voice incredulous. "Actually, scratch that. We're almost to you. You can tell us in person. Have they hurt you?"

"Dragons don't hurt people," Randa countered.

"They haven't hurt me. They're kind of... nice."

"Stay on the phone. We'll be there in two minutes," Vi ordered.

My lips curved upward just the tiniest bit at the normalcy of her giving me an order. She was the head chef at a small restaurant in town, and while she didn't really like her job, she was damn good at it.

I made my way back onto the porch, staying on the phone as I pulled it away from my ear and told Brynn, "My friends tracked me here. They're only a minute away."

She laughed. "I have friends like that too. They'll need to know what's going on."

It seemed like a good sign that she wasn't against me having visitors. And that August wasn't, either. The heat thing was going to be shitty, but at least I wasn't actually in prison.

"My brothers are on their way too. They'll be here in a few hours," August said.

I couldn't stop myself from looking at him.

Or from staring just a little too long.

The sound of Vi's SUV's tires on the dirt ripped my attention back to the road. They parked next to Brynn's Hummer without pause, and Vi was striding toward me a heartbeat later, fire in her eyes.

Not literal fire, like August's, but still.

Randa was behind her. Unlike her sister, her gaze was curious.

Reserved, too.

Both of them were tall, natural blondes with light skin. Randa had a full tattoo sleeve on her right arm, made up of colorful floral designs, so it wasn't difficult to tell them apart, but I didn't struggle with that anyway. Their personalities and the way they carried themselves were too different to mistake them for each other.

Brynn was looking back and forth between the two of them. "And I thought *my* brothers looked alike."

"They're identical twins." I hung up my phone and slipped it in my pocket.

Vi reached the stairs that led up to the porch and glared at all three supernaturals sitting on the wooden planks before looking at me.

August stood, and my attention moved back to him.

I couldn't help it.

He set a hand on my lower back. Because of the fabric separating us, it just felt warm. There was no relief from the tension in my muscles, unfortunately.

Vi looked at me and August as Miranda stepped into place beside her.

He leaned his lips closer to my ear before murmuring, "Don't give them the details. It's against dragon law to share information about our mating process with humans. The thunder will punish us if we break it."

So I had to keep secrets from my best friends.

Awesome.

Great.

Wonderful.

"What happened?" Randa finally asked, her eyes lingering on me.

I had no idea what I was allowed to say, but figured August would hopefully intervene before I blurted anything I shouldn't.

"I'm a dragon shifter, and fate has declared Elodie my potential soulmate," August said, his voice rumbly. The way he said my name made goosebumps break out on my arms. "We won't find out if the bond is genuine for a few weeks. It'll either become permanent at that point, or it will break entirely. Until then, she has to remain with me."

His words were bullshit, but *did* seem reasonably close enough to the truth for my friends.

Or at least, to what I knew to be the truth.

Which also could've been bullshit.

The situation was a mess.

"We're going to need to hear that from her," Vi said, her voice flat.

"That's fine." August gestured me toward them.

I made my way off the porch, wrapping my arms around my middle as I went. Considering I was wearing the dragon's clothes, and *not* wearing a bra or panties, I felt kind of exposed.

Vi started to pull me in for a hug the moment I stepped off the porch, but I held up a hand, wearing a sheepish expression. "He's got this thing with how I smell."

I glanced at him over my shoulder, and he dipped his head.

"Is this seriously some kind of mate thing?" Randa asked, her forehead wrinkling. "I thought dragon shifters took their mates to Mate Mountain."

"Where did you learn that?" Vi asked.

Randa shrugged. "The internet."

"Umm..." I looked back at August again.

"Only if the bond seals permanently."

Ah.

Right.

Sure.

"It's new. I'm still trying to figure everything out," I admitted, looking back at my friends again. "I'm going to have to move here until we deal with the bond thing. The dragons are going to communicate with the school, to make sure I can still graduate on time."

"No one wants to piss off the dragons. I'm sure the university will do whatever he needs them to," Randa said.

"How do you know he's telling the truth?" Vi brought us back to the conversation at hand.

"I can feel it." That much was completely and utterly true. "Fire appeared in his eyes when he touched me, and I felt the change in here." I tapped the center of my chest.

It wasn't my *heart* he had affected, but that was close enough.

After we made it through heat without giving in, and there were no dragons keeping a close eye on me, I'd tell my friends everything. Until then, what choice did I have but to play along?

"This is insane," Vi protested.

"Completely and entirely," I agreed.

"And romantic," Randa offered.

We both flashed her incredulous looks, and she smiled.

Miranda was the artist of the three of us, so it didn't surprise me that she could see the good in the situation. She didn't fit the "moody artist" stereotype even slightly. She was calm, quiet, and more at peace than anyone else I'd ever met.

She threw out, "It is. Everyone knows how supernaturals are with their mates. If your bond becomes permanent, it guarantees devotion and loyalty. How does it get more romantic than that?"

"Ignore her," Vi grumbled. "What are you going to do if he actually becomes your mate?"

"I have no idea," I admitted. "We'll figure it out if we get there, I guess. For now, I'm holding on to the hope that this is all over in a few weeks.

Vi nodded. "What can we do to help?"

"She obviously needs clothes." Randa gestured toward me.

"Yeah, I need a lot of my stuff. I think the semester will end around the time all of this is over with, so there's no point in leaving it at the apartment."

"We'll take care of it," Vi promised.

"Thank you." There was gratitude in my voice. I hoped they knew it was genuine.

Randa stepped closer to me. "All romance aside, do you feel safe with him? You know we can't leave you here if you don't. The last thing we want is a repeat of Dickwad."

I bit my lip.

It hadn't been long enough for me to feel genuinely safe or unsafe with August.

Especially considering he'd mentioned himself *devolving*.

"That's enough of an answer," Vi said. "We're staying."

They couldn't stay, though.

Not when we were dealing with the lust of heat, and lying about the way the magic worked.

So I had to convince them otherwise.

I wasn't a fantastic liar, so I called for help. "Brynn? Can you come here for a second?"

She joined our huddle a moment later, leaning in. "What are we talking about?"

"Elodie dated a vampire a year ago. It ended when he put her in the hospital. What guarantee do we have that this won't go the same way?" Vi asked. As always, she didn't beat around the bush.

Brynn's eyes sharpened. "August would sooner take his own life than physically hurt Elodie. Dragons protect the people that matter to them, period. And until their bond is either broken or cemented, El is at the top of that list. He won't hurt her—and he'll make damn sure no one else does either."

There was a short pause before she added, "It's physically impossible for most supernaturals to hurt their mates. Dragons included. And until the bond is broken, that's exactly what they are."

There was a moment of silence before Randa said, "Well, that settles it. Let's go grab her stuff. Her hair looks sad."

"It does, doesn't it?" I glanced down at the gnarled strands.

"Extremely," Randa agreed.

"Since when do you let people call you El?" Vi asked, looking over at me.

Her anger and worry had deflated with Brynn's words, too. I could only hope they were genuine.

"Since Brynn asked while I was overwhelmed by the fact that I'm temporarily mated to a dragon shifter."

Vi snorted.

Randa smiled. "Or permanently."

"Don't push it," I warned.

She laughed, grabbing Vi's arm. "We'll be back in an hour or two with your things. Love you."

"Love you too."

I was quiet as I watched them climb back in the car and drive away.

"So we have an hour or two to put the house together enough that they won't be worried when they see it," Brynn said.

"Longer. When Randa says an hour or two, it means three or four. We always joke that she does everything as ineffectively as possible. As soon as there's a time-limit on something, she slows way down."

Brynn smiled. "They seem like good friends."

"The best."

A shadow moved over us, and I didn't have to look back to feel August step up behind me. His hand landed on my hip, and the grip felt possessive in a way that made me shiver.

"Tell me Dickwad's name," he said.

"How did you hear that?" I didn't look back at him.

Honestly, I wasn't even surprised he had.

"Shifters have good ears. Give me his name."

"Why?"

"So I can deal with him," August growled.

"A man who would hurt one woman will likely hurt the next. We'll keep an eye on him, and if he tries anything, we'll make sure he can't hurt anyone else," Brynn clarified.

I finally looked over my shoulder at August, and my stomach clenched.

The look on his face... it was complete and utter fury.

If I gave him Dickwad's name, he was going to kill the bastard. And as much as Dickwad deserved it, I didn't want his death on my hands.

But Brynn had a point about keeping an eye on him. I also didn't want another woman's pain on my hands, let alone her life.

So I had to tell Brynn, but couldn't tell August.

I'd have to text it to her later, when I was away from him.

"I don't want you getting involved," I said, my gaze still locked with August's. Seeing the fire in his eyes was really damn weird.

Before he could growl at me again, another vehicle pulled up. This one was a gigantic truck with the name of a furniture store on the side.

I took a seat on the porch again, out of the way of the supernatural guys as they worked with the delivery crew to unload the furniture. August must've decided to let other people in the cabin for the time being, because all of them headed in with the stuff.

While they were all inside, and Brynn was directing them, I sent her a quick message with Dickwad's name. I added a warning for her not to give it to August, too.

She winked at me the next time she stepped back out, and lifted a finger to her lips, telling me she'd keep the secret.

When the guys put a big porch swing a few feet away from me, I couldn't resist the urge to make myself at home on it. I grabbed my bag and took a seat. Though the soreness in my muscles was shitty, I ignored it as I opened my laptop and tried to focus on my project again.

I got distracted every now and then—mostly by the feeling of August's gaze on me as he headed toward or walked away from the house. But for the most part, I managed to get things done.

A grocery delivery van came while they were still unloading the furniture, and Brynn took over organizing those. I offered to help her, but she waved her hand and told me to keep working, so I did.

Another truck showed up with more furniture around the time they finished with the first, and we said goodbye to the grocery delivery people.

It seemed like way too much furniture to me, but I hadn't actually walked around to see the whole cabin, so I didn't know how big it was. And I noticed a few rugs and fake plants being carried in during my moments of distraction, so it seemed safe to assume they weren't just furnishing it —they were decorating it, too.

I just stayed on the porch swing and kept working.

five

ELODIE

EVENTUALLY, the last furniture truck drove away.

I could faintly hear Brynn and Bash talking as they did something inside the house. I wasn't sure where August was, but he wasn't outside, so I was finally alone.

Or alone*ish*.

The ache in my muscles was still getting worse, though.

And I was definitely sweating.

I kept hoping that focusing on my project would distract me from heat's magic, but it hadn't.

Vi and Randa showed up again after a bit longer, with all of my stuff. They'd packed it in the set of pink rolling suitcases and matching duffel bag I'd picked out before my freshman year in college. The suitcases had seen better days, but they'd survived years of flying back home for all of the major holidays.

I didn't talk with my older brother and sister much, but I was close with my parents. My mom, mainly. We chatted on the phone a few times a week, and she was definitely one of my closest friends.

I had no idea how I was going to tell her about heat.

And August.

It would probably be best if I just kept my mouth shut until after we made it through without sealing the bond, but I didn't know if I'd manage keeping the truth from her for that long. I was a terrible liar. And if we ever did a video call, which we did often, she would definitely notice that I was living somewhere new. My little apartment was nowhere near as pretty as August's cabin.

"Hey!" Randa smiled, a duffel bag hanging off one of her shoulders and the handle of a beat-up pink suitcase in her opposite hand.

I set my laptop down on the porch swing and headed toward them.

"I still think this is a bad idea," Vi warned, hauling two suit-cases herself.

"If there was a way out, I would've already taken it." I grabbed the biggest suitcase from Vi and the duffel from Randa on our way in.

It took major self-control not to stop in my tracks when I saw the newly-furnished living room.

There was a soft rug on the floor, with a comfortable-looking sectional positioned on the edge of it.

August was mounting a TV on the wall, with a drill in his hand.

I had a hard time looking away from him, too.

The kitchen had been furnished with barstools, plus a table and chairs. All of them were in dark colors that made the purposefully-rugged wood cabinets stand out more.

There were pictures of the mountains on the walls, soft-looking blankets draped artfully over the couch, and decorations placed perfectly around the room. The combination made it look cozy, but classy too.

"Wow," Vi remarked.

"It's beautiful," Randa agreed, her eyes still moving over the room.

"Not a terrible place to wait for our mating bond to break, right?" I tried to make myself sound somewhat cheerful, but totally failed.

And I still hadn't managed to peel my gaze off August, so I didn't know if they were even paying attention to me.

"Your room's across the hall from mine," August said, looking over his shoulder at us.

The way his eyes moved up and down my figure made me feel even hotter.

Hopefully Vi and Randa had packed my deodorant, because I was going to need it.

...and my birth control pills.

Condoms too, maybe?

August had made it sound like everything other than penis-in-vagina sex was going to go down, so actually, we could forget the condoms. I'd stay on the birth control just in case, though.

"Thanks," I said, and led them down the hallway.

August's was at the far end on the right, but there were a few more doors on the way. Vi and Randa peeked inside of all of them, discovering a furnished spare room, two hall closets with a vacuum, a few blankets, and some extra sheets. The one on the left, before August's door, was mine.

It was decorated just like the rest of the house, with mountain landscapes on the walls. The furniture was dark wood, the bed was massive, and the comforter was a soft white duvet. The bedding was all light and airy, and there were so many pillows it was ridiculous.

If I hadn't been sweating so damn much, I would've thought it looked really welcoming.

But I was sweating.

An ice bath sounded more comfortable to me.

Or maybe an ice cream cone...

"At least you'll be comfortable here. This place is gorgeous," Vi said.

Randa left my suitcase at the foot of the bed and stepped over to the large windows, pulling the curtains back. "Wow, look at this view." There was thick appreciation in her voice. "I want a dragon shifter."

"You can have this one after our bond breaks," I drawled.

Vi snorted, and Randa laughed.

My stomach clenched, though.

Despite my words, I didn't like the thought of her with August. It made me nauseous to even consider it.

The reaction was bizarre, but I didn't let myself overthink it. It was probably another part of heat.

"I can move into the spare room down the hall if you want," Vi said. "To make sure you're safe."

"He won't hurt me." Despite my uncertainty, I was starting to actually believe that. Brynn had eased whatever lingering fear I had after seeing them argue outside the coffee shop. "And you'd be way too far from the restaurant. Plus, I don't think August would agree with it."

"He probably wants you all to himself," Randa teased.

"You are way too on-board with this," Vi grumbled at her.

"We need to talk about something normal. I feel like I'm losing my mind here," I said, as I unzipped my first suitcase and started unpacking my things.

Though Vi was reluctant, they both filled me in on what I'd missed. Randa told us about her classes that morning, and Vi told us about her shift at the restaurant the night before.

When they finally headed out, leaving me with massive hugs and promises to kill August if he did anything wrong, I felt slightly more at ease.

Only slightly, though.

And *wow*, I was uncomfortably hot. The underboob sweat was driving me insane.

I would've put on a bra as soon as I unpacked, but I knew August thought all my stuff smelled like my friends. If I put any of it on, he'd just tell me to take another shower.

As soon as they were gone, I grabbed my laptop off the porch and headed back into the kitchen. August and Bash were lifting the gigantic TV onto the wall mount, and my gaze immediately landed on the blond dragon.

I couldn't help but stop and watch.

His tight ass...

Those massive thighs...

Yum.

Just yum.

Maybe Randa had a point about wanting a dragon shifter. Or any supernatural, really.

I'd only been with Dickwad for a few months, and much of the relationship had been a toxic mess, but we'd had enough sex to ruin me for human guys. I hadn't even attempted to hook up with anyone since I left him.

"If you're staring at the demon, you know I'll have to kill him, Fireball," August grumbled.

"She's staring at *you*, asshole," Brynn shot back from the kitchen. My gaze jerked to hers, and she winked at me. "I'm the only one checking out Bash."

The guys made sure the TV was on the mount's rails properly, then stepped back.

"This place looks amazing," I admitted, forcing myself to look around the open living room and kitchen area.

"We paid the furniture store for some of their floor models with all the decorations," Brynn said with a grin.

"Their designers have good taste, then."

She nodded. "I threw some stuff together for dinner, to make your lives easier. You'll just need to stick it in the oven. The instructions are on your grocery list."

Apparently, we had a grocery list.

It was too weird to think of there being an *us* for the grocery list thing to seem that odd.

"Thank you."

"Any time. And since you already smell like your friends..." She crossed the room and pulled me in for a massive hug. "Our other brothers should be getting here soon. Jasper and Eli. They're with some other members of the thunder—

which is a group of dragons, like a wolf pack almost. They'll be pissed if they find us here, so we have to go, but you have my number. Use it. I will if you don't. Welcome to the family."

"Temporarily," I reminded her, though I returned her hug.

"Once a Sky, always a Sky." She finally released me and stepped back. I hadn't known their last name was Sky, but thought it was kind of funny, considering they were dragons. "Ready, Crash?"

I blinked at the name.

His name was *Bash*, wasn't it?

"Yup." The demon wrapped his arm around her waist, tucking her against his side and kissing her forehead before they headed out. "Good luck fighting fate," he called over his shoulder. "For your sakes, I hope you're better at it than I was."

My gaze flicked between them, my curiosity suddenly sky-high.

August followed them to the door, and I couldn't help but do the same. Peering past him, I watched Bash lift Brynn into their Hummer before he walked around to the driver's side.

"What happened between them?" I asked August, who was already looking at me instead of them.

"I left her at his place so he would keep her safe while I went home to deal with the thunder. He fucked her, instead."

I rolled my eyes. "I'm sure there was more to it than that."

He forced his attention back to the now-empty dirt road. "His brother mated with one of her best friends, so they were around each other fairly often. He fought the urge to make her his mate for around a year. When she found out, she made it her mission in life to talk him into sealing their bond. After a while, she succeeded. They've been inseparable since."

"Wow." I had to respect a woman willing to fight for what she wanted. "How long ago was that?"

"Four or five years." He slipped his hands into his pockets. "You need to shower again before the thunder gets here."

"Why are they coming at all?"

"It's a long story."

I waited.

He let out a long breath. "Jasper, Eli, and I raised Brynn. We're protective of her. The thunder found out that I made a deal with the demons to keep her safe, and they want to punish me for it. I'm supposed to be on my way to prison right now. Jas took my place as the leader last week."

My eyes widened. "*What?*"

"The conversation you interrupted was me saying goodbye to my sister. She was trying to convince me to refuse the rest of the dragons."

My horror grew. "They want to put you in the supernatural prison? Isn't it full of violent criminals?"

"Yep." His gaze remained trained on the forest. "When they see that we're genuinely in heat, they'll assign me a guard to stay outside. If we seal the bond, you'll end up in prison with me."

"Holy *shit*."

"I won't let it happen."

"You said *everyone* seals the bond, August."

"Everyone but us."

I shook my head, raking a hand through the top of my hair a little desperately. "I would not survive in a supernatural jail."

"I know," he growled, finally looking at me again. "I won't let them lock you up."

I let out an unsteady breath. "I'm going to put some of my clothes in the wash, then shower. I'll be quick."

"Don't worry about them. If the bastards have to wait, they'll wait."

I would hurry anyway.

The last thing I needed was a bunch of pissed-off dragons hating me for taking a long shower.

It only took me a minute to grab a few sets of my clothes and start them in the washer. Showering was almost as fast. I got to use my own soap and shampoo, thankfully. And the cold water helped a little with the sweating.

As I dried off, I realized I needed another set of August's clothes. Reluctantly, I called for him.

He came striding back in, his gaze immediately landing on my towel-clad figure. Despite it being the second time he'd seen me like that, his gaze was hot.

Hungry, too.

"I need another set of your clothes until mine are washed and dried," I said.

"You can have them any time you want." His voice was low.

It nearly made me shiver.

"Thanks." He stared at me for another moment, then finally peeled his shirt over his head.

"What are you doing?"

"Giving you my clothes."

"I didn't ask for the ones you're *wearing*."

"This shirt smells like me."

"I don't need to smell like you. I washed off, just like you asked—now, I just want some clean clothes."

His nostrils flared. "You reek of flowers."

"Flowers smell good!"

"Like hell they do." He put the shirt in my hand. "Wear this. I'll find you a clean pair of my boxers."

With that, he stormed off.

I resisted the urge to throw his shirt at his head as he did.

HE BROUGHT me boxers that looked and smelled clean, so I decided not to argue anymore, and just put them on. He'd found a fresh shirt to wear himself, so I couldn't ogle his chest, either.

When I was dressed, I carried my laptop back out to the porch. August was in the kitchen, wiping everything down with some kind of cleaning solution, when I walked by.

Maybe he really *was* sensitive to smells.

Curiosity got the best of me.

After I sat down, I lifted the collar of his shirt to my nose and inhaled lightly.

Nope, didn't smell anything.

And I'd put on a ton of deodorant, so hopefully that remained true even though I'd already started sweating.

I worked on my project for a bit, before the gleam of silver caught my eyes.

When I looked up, I saw a dragon in the sky.

A few dragons.

One...

Two...

Three...

Four...

Five.

Five dragons.

Two silvers, a red, a blue, and a green. They were insanely shiny, and still high enough above me that I couldn't tell how big they were compared to me.

I didn't trust August, but I felt more comfortable with him than I did with five gigantic, fire-breathing strangers.

"August!" I called out.

He was on the porch a heartbeat later, immediately looking to the sky. He barely glanced at them before focusing on me. "Jasper and Eli are leading the group. The others are some of the most difficult dragons we have. Gordon, Kev, and Lox."

"Okay."

"You'll stay on the porch while I talk to them. One of them will come up here to check your temperature, but other than that, don't interact with them. And for the love of the damn sky, don't stare at them. I'm in enough hot water with the thunder without killing someone because you're attracted to them."

"Why do you care who I'm attracted to?"

He leaned a little closer. "You're mine for the next few weeks, Fireball. Mine. Got it?"

"Screw off," I whispered, though my eyes were locked with his.

His lips curved upward.

The wind picked up around us, and I closed my laptop.

The dragons were landing.

August's chest rumbled in annoyance, and he stepped in front of me so I couldn't see them shift.

I dropped my laptop on the porch swing and stood up, trying to move around him so I could see. I caught sight of a flash of bare skin before his gigantic hand landed on my hip, and he yanked me behind him.

"Are they *naked*?" I called over the rushing wind.

"Clothes don't shift with us."

Guess that was a yes.

And suddenly, I understood why he'd tried to stop me from looking at them. If it pissed him off when I glanced at a guy who was wearing clothes, I didn't want to know what he'd do if I checked out some other naked guy.

Especially if the naked guy happened to be his brother.

The wind died down.

"I changed my mind. You're staying with me," he grumbled. "Put your hands on my waist."

"I really don't want to—"

"It wasn't a request, Fireball. Hands on my waist."

I huffed, but did as he'd commanded.

His body was strong beneath my fingers, like the man was made out of stone. He didn't feel warm to me, given my ridiculously-sweaty self, but he still felt good.

A tiny, itty-bitty part of me wished he hadn't found another shirt, so I could've put my hands on his bare skin.

I wasn't about to acknowledge that part, though.

"Did they bring pants?" I asked, my voice muffled against his back.

"No."

So there were five hot, naked supernatural men in what was basically my new front yard.

Lovely.

"Should I be scared?" I asked, not *feeling* scared.

Mostly, I just felt like my hands were on the sexiest man alive.

But I was ignoring that, too.

"No. I won't let them hurt you, and if they try, my brothers will take my side."

So it would be three to three. Not great odds, but good enough that I didn't have to worry, at least.

"Great," I said.

His hand remained on my hip as he walked down the porch steps, still holding me close enough to his back that he could catch me if I stumbled.

Then again, I'd probably just fall right into his back if I tripped.

And I'd probably like it.

Sigh.

We made our way out to the guys. I saw five shadows around the same heights and size, and thankfully, none of the shadows showed anything steamy.

Figuratively or literally.

"Well, it *looks* like you started heat," a masculine voice said, with humor. It reminded me of August's.

"Shut up, Eli," another guy grumbled. His voice didn't sound like August's.

"The fire in his eyes is enough evidence. Gordon, check her skin," a third man said. Like the first, he sounded similar to August. I had to think those two were probably his brothers.

My skin?

August had said they'd need to take my temperature somehow.

One of the shadows moved, and a guy stepped up in front of August. August's hand snapped out, blocking him before he could get any closer to me. "Reach up, Elodie."

It was weird hearing him use my name.

Maybe I didn't mind the nickname as much as I'd thought.

I lifted my hand above August's shoulder.

"Two fingers, for three seconds. Touch her any longer and I snap your wrist." August's voice was low, and more gravelly than I'd ever heard it.

Goosebumps spread over my arms.

It was kind of sexy when he protected me like that.

Not that I could admit it, of course. If he asked, it was unsexy.

Un.

Sexy.

Two fingers pressed to the inside of my wrist.

I counted silently.

One.

Two.

Three.

His fingers were gone before I finished.

"She's hotter than any of us," Gordon said.

It sounded like he was hitting on me, so it didn't surprise me at all when August growled at him.

His shadow moved again as he backed away, and I saw his hands raise.

"We can all accept that we're not imprisoning a pair of potential mates going through heat, as much as August might deserve it, right?" one of his brothers said.

Probably Jasper, since Eli had sounded more playful the last time he spoke.

A few of them agreed grudgingly.

"Gordon will stay here to keep an eye on August. Eli will too, to make sure he doesn't lose his mind to heat as they try to resist it," Jasper said. "Understood?"

When they all voiced their agreement, two of the guys shifted and took to the sky. The green and red dragons.

I couldn't stop my eyes from following them. I'd never seen a dragon up close. They were both gorgeous and terrifying at the same time.

"Good luck fighting the bond," Jasper said, before he shifted too. He was one of the silver ones, so I assumed Eli was the other.

"Did you buy a cabin for me?" Eli checked.

"Of course I did," August grumbled. "It's a few miles north. Red roof."

Apparently money wasn't an issue for them.

"Thanks. We'll get settled, and come by in the morning to officially meet your female. You've got at least a few days before you lose your mind completely."

With that, he and Gordon flew off too.

I made a noise of irritation at him calling me *"your female"*, and August let out a long breath, finally turning around to face me.

Our bodies almost brushed, but didn't.

That was for the best, because I didn't need him reminding me that his touch could make me stop sweating and hurting.

"I want to see your brother's dragon form up close when he comes back," I said, instead of protesting the ownership-claiming thing that kept happening.

August's eyes narrowed. "The only dragon you're meeting up close is me, Fireball."

"Then I want to see *your* dragon form up close in the morning."

He grunted.

It wasn't a yes, but it wasn't a no, either.

We started toward the cabin, and he reached the door before me. Instead of going inside, he grabbed my laptop off the porch.

Though I wanted to be irritated that he'd picked it up, I was pretty sure he'd done so just to be nice.

To prove my suspicion, he handed it to me before he pulled the door open and gestured me inside.

"Thanks," I said.

"Of course." His voice was calmer than it had been a few moments earlier.

I stepped past him, suddenly hit with a wave of uncertainty.

It was the middle of the afternoon, and we were alone together, in a secluded cabin.

It was just me and August.

How was I supposed to act?

What was I supposed to feel?

"I'm going back to cleaning," August said. "This place smells awful."

I sniffed the air. "I don't smell anything."

"You're not a shifter." His hand brushed my side lightly before he strode back into the kitchen, where he'd left his cleaning solution.

Though I didn't think it was necessary, his cleaning did clear the air a bit. So, I headed to the couch and opened up my computer. I threw myself back into my project, and the lingering awkwardness vanished.

six

ELODIE

I SAT on the couch and cursed heat while I worked. August cleaned every possible surface with his unscented multipurpose solution.

Countertops.

Tables.

Chairs.

The fridge.

The TV.

Doorknobs.

Walls.

He stopped long enough to put our dinner in the oven, then went back to cleaning.

When he came over to the couch with his spray, I gave him a warning look. "I don't think you're supposed to use that on fabric."

"It'll survive."

Without further ado, he sprayed it, wiping at it pointlessly —and roughly—with his towel.

I eyed him as his hands and spray bottle neared my backside.

My body ached too much to get up. He'd just have to go around me.

My ass was probably wet with sweat, too. I was so damn miserable.

August didn't so much as pause, though. He dropped his spray bottle and towel on the couch in one motion, and scooped me and my computer up into his arms in another.

I would've protested, if the motion hadn't put his skin on mine.

In less than a heartbeat, all the soreness in my muscles vanished.

The warmth, too.

Instead of setting me down on the floor or the wet part of the couch, he narrowed his eyes at me. "You're sweating."

He'd felt the sweat on the backs of my thighs.

Well, that was embarrassing.

"I'm fine," I said.

Was I blushing?

Yup.

Blushing hard.

Why had society made sweat such a taboo thing? Everyone sweats!

Then again, most people didn't sweat in an air-conditioned room in the middle of the mountains.

That was all heat's doing.

The butt sweat, the thigh sweat, the underboob sweat... shudder.

"I didn't ask if you were okay. I said you're sweating."

"You sent me into heat, remember? Pretty sure heat equals sweating."

"It does. But if you're feeling symptoms, you need to tell me. I can't feel what you're feeling. I don't know if you're hot, or in pain."

"I told you, I'm fine. You don't need to hold me like this."

He scowled, but carried me into the kitchen and set me down at the table. "When you get hot or start feeling pain, say something."

"Alright."

It wasn't the truth.

I'd stay quiet until I had melted into a puddle of sweat, or the pain was bad enough to make me feel like I'd been stabbed. Not because I was a martyr. Because I was a stubborn bitch, and I wasn't about to throw myself into August's arms.

If I jumped into his arms, I wouldn't want to leave until heat was over.

And I was *not* going to prison because I couldn't resist sleeping with some gorgeous supernatural guy.

The pain was survivable.

It would have to be.

He continued cleaning the couch, then disappeared into one of the rooms.

"I don't want all-purpose spray on my bedding!" I called over my shoulder. "I'll throw it in the wash if it smells bad!"

"Alright."

A few minutes later, I heard the washer door open.

I'd forgotten to switch the laundry.

Whoops.

"I'll switch it," I added.

"I'm already doing it."

A minute later, I heard the dryer start. The washer followed.

When he made it back into the kitchen, I apologized quickly.

"I'm sorry. You shouldn't have to clean up after me. I should've set a timer."

He flashed me an irritated look. "I'm the reason you're stuck here, Fireball. I can handle a few chores."

Well, then.

He wasn't wrong.

"A *thank you* is better than an apology most of the time," August said, pulling the oven door open to check on the food.

"I'll keep that in mind."

The food must not have been done, because he headed back into the bedrooms to start disinfecting things again.

I worked a bit more, but he came back after ten minutes or so.

"Is your sense of smell really good enough to bother wiping down the fabric couch?" I asked him, more curious than anything else.

"Not usually."

I waited for him to clarify, but he didn't.

He hadn't responded poorly to me pushing or asking questions yet, so I figured it was worth a shot.

"What does that mean?"

"My sense of smell is only slightly better than a human's most of the time. Mating is the only thing that changes it."

"How does it change?"

"Some kinds of lizards have something on the roof of their mouth that helps their sense of smell. Dragons have them too—but they're only active as far as our mates go. It's a mesh between tasting and smelling. Supposedly, I'll be able to tell your needs apart based on your smell when I get used to it. Right now, all the scents in the house are making it impossible and driving me insane."

"Damn."

"Yup." He opened the oven door to check on the food again.

I guess he was satisfied with how it looked, because he pulled it out a minute later, without bothering to grab oven mitts.

My eyebrows raised in alarm, but he showed no sign that his skin was burning.

Guess it made sense for dragons to be fireproof.

He dished up food for us, then grabbed glasses of water and filled them before joining me at the table.

We ate in relative silence. The food was great, so I'd have to text Brynn to thank her.

When we were done eating, August put the dishes in the dishwasher without so much as suggesting I should do it. I stayed at the table and went back to work while he returned to his beloved multi-purpose spray.

Soon enough, he swapped his spray for a vacuum.

When my blankets were clean and dry, I retreated to my room with a murmured goodnight, locking my door and tucking myself into bed.

My body ached horribly.

The sweating was insane.

I ended up throwing the blankets to the foot of the bed, and changing into a clean tank top and a pair of the cheeky panties I preferred. The rest of my clothes, and August's, could screw off.

I tried to fall asleep, but couldn't.

Instead, I spent the night tossing, turning, and wincing with just about every motion.

I might have heard rhythmic footsteps in the hallway throughout the night. Part of me was positive August was pacing out there in the early hours of the morning.

The other part of me thought I was just hallucinating because I couldn't sleep.

It took a hell of a lot of effort to stop myself from going out there to see if he was actually walking around...

And even more effort to convince myself that climbing into bed with him wasn't the answer to my problems.

He was the cure for my discomfort.

But I couldn't embrace it. Not yet. I still wasn't sure what I wanted to do about the whole mate thing.

So, I stayed in bed, cursing myself and the situation I'd landed in. And wishing I had listened to Brynn's conversation with her brother before assuming she was in danger and interrupting.

THAT NIGHT FELT LIKE A YEAR.

When I finally shuffled out of my room around five AM, I stopped in the hallway.

August was at the end of it, shirtless, messy-haired, and wearing just a pair of sweats.

He was insanely gorgeous.

And it looked like he really had been pacing.

His eyes dipped to my tits.

Mine did too.

Yeah, I hadn't changed out of the tank top and panties. The tank was white, damp with my sweat, and definitely see-through. The navy-blue panties offered coverage, at least.

I looked back at his eyes, and found them blazing brightly. The look on his face was intense in a way I'd never seen from him, or any other man.

And he was still looking at my very-visible-nipples.

The rest of my body, too.

I'd never felt so sexy in my life.

A new wave of heat rolled down my spine, and my back arched a little with the discomfort.

"You're in pain," he growled, finally looking at my eyes.

"I'm fine," I whispered.

If I'd spoken any louder, I was pretty sure my voice would crack.

It had been a long, long night, and lack of sleep always made me feel emotional.

He crossed the space between us in three long steps, but I held up a hand before he touched me.

He stopped abruptly when I did.

That alone told me I could trust him to respect my body, at least.

"Yes, I'm in pain," I said quietly. "And sweating like a fiend. It sucks, but I'm surviving."

His jaw clenched.

The fire in his eyes burned brighter.

But he finally jerked his head in a nod. "I'll fight the need to soothe you as long as I can."

"Thank you."

I stepped past him, grabbing my laptop off the kitchen table and slipping out to the porch. It was cool enough outside to make me feel a little better. And hey, at least I'd have a good view out there while I suffered.

Since August had already seen my nipples and underwear, I didn't bother putting more clothes on yet. I was miserable enough in what I had on. Wearing more fabric would only make that worse.

I opened my laptop and tried to work on my project, but failed. My mind was so fuzzy, it was practically spinning. Focusing was impossible.

Half an hour and absolutely zero progress later, I closed my laptop again and lifted my thighs to my chest. My heels dug in to the bottom of the porch swing, and I hugged my knees close.

Tears stung my eyes.

I hated crying, and rarely did so—but between the discomfort and lack of sleep, fighting the emotions was useless.

I was exhausted.

I was sweaty.

I was horny.

Why was I even resisting the urge to let August soothe me?

Sometime during the night, I'd forgotten. Maybe there had never been a reason.

He clearly wasn't Dickwad. He hadn't shown any sign of violence, and dragons were protectors.

The smell of something cooking hit my nose. Pancakes, maybe?

I was too tired to get up and check, or look around.

I wanted to call my friends. To tell them the truth. To hear someone tell me that I was stronger than I felt, and that I was going to be okay. But even if I could, I wasn't sure I would actually ask for help or comfort.

Usually, I dealt with difficult things on my own.

I took in a shaky breath, then watched the sun rise over the forest and forced myself to reconsider my situation. I wiped away my tears as they fell, but there was no stopping them. Once the flood gates were open, it was nearly impossible to close them again.

I was trapped in a cabin with a dragon shifter. We were going through a magical mating process that would make me horny and uncomfortable if I tried to maintain distance between us.

He seemed like a decent enough guy, considering he'd raised his baby sister and protected her no matter the cost.

Plus, he respected me when I told him not to touch me.

And he was gorgeous. Insanely so.

Sleeping with him definitely wouldn't be a hardship. Pun not intended.

Hell, it could even be fun.

He'd made it sound like heat's magic was pushing him to make my pleasure and comfort a priority, so what was the point in staying away from him?

If I had to choose between pain and misery, or hot sex, the answer seemed pretty obvious.

August came out of the house soon enough, carrying two plates loaded with bacon, pancakes, and syrup. It smelled good, but my stomach was too twisted to be hungry.

"Is that seat open?" He looked at the space next to me, where my laptop was currently sitting.

I nodded, moving my computer to the porch floor.

August didn't mention the crying, thankfully.

He sat down beside me, and his arm brushed mine.

I inhaled sharply as the heat and soreness vanished instantly, and I leaned against him a little more as I lowered my feet back to the porch.

He set a plate on top of my thighs, sliding closer until we were pressed together.

The relief was incredible.

And with my discomfort gone, I was suddenly hungry.

Ravenously, painfully hungry.

I cleaned my overflowing plate quickly. It was nearly twice as much as I would usually eat, but I didn't let myself consider that. My mind was feeling clearer and stronger with every bite.

"The heat's magic is hard on your body. You'll need to eat more than usual," August said. "Especially if we're fighting it."

"How much worse is it going to get?" I asked.

He was silent for a beat.

It was long enough for me to sigh in response.

"This is still the beginning, Fireball. Right now, the magic just wants us touching."

Eventually, it would want us having sex.

I bit my lip. "How are we going to do it?"

"Not like this."

He took my empty plate, stacked it on his, and set them both on the wooden planks at his feet.

When he draped an arm lightly over my shoulder, I couldn't stop myself from leaning closer. Not just because of the relief from pain, but because he was strong.

Steady.

Calm, too.

The sunrise was much prettier when I was with him like that.

A few minutes passed before either of us spoke again.

"What's our best chance?" I asked him.

August didn't answer right away.

He took a moment to really consider it, which I appreciated.

Finally, he said, "If you keep trying to deal with it on your own, you're going to end up curled in a ball of agony. I'll keep fighting my instincts, but knowing you're in pain makes it much harder. We'll make it a week or two, but I'll eventually break, and you'll be so desperate for relief that you'll beg me to take you."

Despite his words, his voice was neutral. He didn't seem to want me begging, and he didn't want to lose control.

"What's the alternative?"

"We become a team."

"What?"

He explained, "If we rely on each other, we can retain control for as long as possible, and we'll be more likely to make it through."

"How do we do that?"

"We satisfy the magic."

I blinked.

The magic wanted us to have sex and seal the bond. Weren't we fighting it to *avoid* that outcome?

"Not by making it permanent," he said, as if reading my mind. "We satisfy it like this." He pulled me a little closer, and I remembered that his arm was around my shoulder. It felt so right, I had stopped noticing it somehow.

"By touching?"

"For now, yes. The magic wants us touching, so we touch. We can do so as friends. Sitting together while you work. Sleeping in the same bed, with pillows between us if that's what will make you comfortable. When the magic pushes for more, we give it more."

"How much more?" I countered.

"From what I understand, the next thing it will do is push us to touch more intimately. I can give you that without sealing the bond, and take care of my needs myself. At that point, we just have to retain a shred of control to stop ourselves from taking it all the way."

My face warmed, but not because of the heat.

We were practically strangers, and we were talking about sex casually. While we sat on the porch swing and watched the sunrise. It was bizarre, but not wrong. If anything, it was exactly right, because it was what the bond wanted from us.

"So you're proposing friends with benefits?" I asked.

"Sounds about right."

I'd come to the same conclusion myself, and stopped crying, thankfully. "It would be less shitty than trying to muscle our way through it on our own, I guess. And it has a better potential outcome."

"Yup."

"Alright, I'm in. We're a couple for the next four weeks. Practically attached to each other. It'll be fun."

He chuckled. "*Fun* isn't the word I'd use, Fireball."

I couldn't hold back a smile.

It really could be fun.

seven

AUGUST

"I NEED a shower before your brother shows up," Elodie said, stretching her arms out in front of her.

It took every ounce of my self control not to stare at her tits as the motion pressed them together, lifting the heavy curve of them toward me.

I wanted them in my mouth.

She was the sexiest thing I'd ever seen, in that sheer white tank top and those dark panties. She had to change before my brother showed up, or I'd lose my damn mind.

"How do you want to handle showering?" I asked her.

"I don't know. How do *you* want to handle it?"

That was a loaded question if I'd ever heard one.

I wanted to *handle* the shower with her in my arms.

Her breasts in my hands.

My cock buried inside her.

My teeth in her skin, marking her as mine.

"I haven't thought about it," I lied.

I wasn't going to act on my desires, so the truth didn't seem all that important in the moment.

Elodie considered it. Her dark, wavy hair was a mess, and still smelled annoyingly like flowers. I wanted her scent in my nose, but she seemed determined to hide it from me.

I wanted my hands in her hair just as much.

And her back arching while I devoured her mouth, or her—

"You can stand outside the shower," she decided. "I'll reach out and touch you when the pain gets worse."

It sounded like torture, but I agreed.

I grabbed the plates, and she picked up her laptop. My free arm wrapped around her waist as we headed inside, and she tugged her top up, exposing her bare hip so I could touch her skin.

My cock strained against my sweats as I squeezed her soft waist.

I should've kept my jeans on.

At least they would've hidden my erection a little.

"Your touch doesn't do anything for me if it's over my clothes," she explained to me, as we headed for the kitchen.

Her laptop went back on the table, and I abandoned the dishes in the sink.

"It's not a hardship for me to touch your skin," I said.

She flashed me an amused look. "I sat on your lap in the Hummer, remember? I know exactly how much of a *hardship* I am for you."

I chuckled, and her gaze dipped to my erection, fighting against my sweats. She bit her lip, and her scent changed slightly.

I wasn't well-enough acquainted with her smell to know exactly what the change was, but I assumed it had something to do with her desire.

Or maybe I just hoped for that.

I was losing my mind.

We made it to the bathroom, and she started the water after gesturing for me to turn around. I did, and couldn't help but look down when her clothes hit the floor beside me.

The shower's door was made of glass, so she was going to want me facing away from her the whole time. It'd give a new meaning to the term *cruel and unusual punishment*.

"Does the house smell better to you now?" she asked me, as she stepped under the water.

"A little. I need to open the windows, to air out the smell of the cleaning solution."

"And then you'll be able to smell me better?" She stumbled over the words, and I knew the concept was still strange to her. Hell, it was still strange to me, and I'd known about it my whole life.

"In theory."

"Why in theory?"

"The scent of your shampoo and shower gel is strong."

"Oh." There was a pause.

A long, drawn-out pause.

"I'll survive," I finally said, not wanting to lose the ground we'd gained on the porch.

"I didn't realize it was that big of a deal. Does it bother you?"

Constantly.

"A bit," I said.

"Liar." She was quiet for a moment. The shower's door opened, and her slick hand landed on my bare shoulder.

My cock throbbed painfully, but her soft sigh told me the contact soothed her. That alone made the temptation worth it.

Her hand lingered on my skin. "Go get your unscented stuff. I can look online for something that doesn't smell as strong."

"It bothered you last time."

"My hair doesn't like it," she agreed. "But I'll just tie it up until whatever I order arrives. My mom is a hair stylist; she'll probably have an idea about what I should buy. Or a few bottles she can send me."

"Are you sure?"

She squeezed my shoulder lightly.

I closed my eyes and let out a long breath, struggling against the need to wrap my hand around my cock.

"Yes, I'm sure."

"Alright. Thank you."

"You don't need to thank me. We're a team, remember?"

Maybe that was a bad idea.

It was our best shot... but still.

The more I was around her, the harder it would be to walk away.

Pun not intended.

I stepped away long enough to grab the unscented shit in my bathroom, then headed back.

I froze in the doorway when I reached the bathroom, my gaze landing on my female's bare figure.

Her hands were in her hair, her head tipped back.

The curve of her ass called my name, and the heavy weight of her tits made my cock throb harder.

She felt my eyes on her and turned her head. Her lips curved upward when she saw me staring. "You always look at me like that."

"Like what?"

"I don't know. Intensely."

"Like I want to fuck you?"

She bit her lip.

I crossed the bathroom, stopping when I reached her clothes. Her eyes widened slightly, dilating when I picked up her panties and lifted them to my nose.

I inhaled her scent deeply, and she made a small noise.

My chest rumbled.

I nearly filled my fucking sweats.

"You like the way I smell?" she asked.

"You tell me, Fireball."

Her gaze lowered to my erection, and her face flushed. "What do I smell like?"

"The sky."

The answer left me before I could consider the word.

She blinked.

That probably didn't sound sexy.

"The sky is a rush. Dragons don't look for mates, because

we can't fly without them after we're paired off. Flying is freedom, adrenaline, fun... it's not an insult. I love the sky."

She frowned. "What do you mean, you can't fly without them?"

I let out a harsh breath, tucking her panties in my pocket and stepping closer to the shower. She opened the door long enough to take the shower gel, then set her hand on my shoulder.

With her naked body in front of me, and her hand on my bare shoulder, it took everything I had not to step in there with her.

"Dragons like to keep secrets," she said after a moment.

"Secrets protect us."

"You don't need protection from me, August."

She had no idea.

"Let's make a deal," Elodie said.

"What kind of a deal?"

"We're supposed to be a team now, right?"

I jerked my head in a nod.

"Well, you're so horny you can't think straight."

It was my turn to blink.

The woman wasn't wrong.

"And I'm tired of all the mate-related secrets you're keeping. So why don't we even the playing field? You get in the shower with me, and I'll touch you while you tell me the things you'd rather keep quiet."

My entire body clenched.

How was I supposed to turn that down?

"An hour ago, you didn't even want me to touch you, Fireball." My voice was strained.

"An hour ago, I was sweaty and hurting. You fixed it for me, and we agreed to be a team. This is me keeping up my side of the bargain. And besides, it's not any more of a *hardship* for me to touch you than it is for you to touch me. I've never been more turned-on in my life."

I inhaled deeply, desperate to have the scent of her desire embedded in my lungs, my mouth, my throat. Hell, I wanted it laced through every fiber of my being.

The water concealed it from me, and I nearly snarled in frustration.

"Do we have a deal?" Elodie checked.

"Yes." I stepped out of my pants.

The way her eyes locked on my erection made me throb again.

And again.

She opened the shower's door wider, and I stepped inside.

She took a step back, pressing her ass to the tiled wall.

I gritted my teeth against the urge to sink to my knees in front of her and finally get her taste in my mouth. To watch her unravel on my tongue. To hear her sounds of pleasure.

When I stepped closer, shutting the shower's door behind me, her hand slid over my abdomen. Hot water fell over my head and down my body, but I didn't feel it. Not with her touching my skin.

Elodie's fingers slowly traced the dips and crevices of my abs. "Dragons can't fly without their mates?"

I lifted one of my hands to the shower wall beside her head, and captured her hip with the other. If I didn't occupy them, they'd make their way to her breasts and ass, and she hadn't said I could touch her.

"No. After a dragon takes a mate—or begins a female's heat —he can't fly without her. It's physically impossible. If he tries to take to the sky without her on his back, the magic ricochets, and he automatically shifts back to his human form."

"So you can't fly without me right now?"

"No. When heat ends, I'll have my wings again."

Her finger dragged down the center of my abdomen, and my body clenched as she slowly found my cock.

My lips twisted in a snarl as her soft hand wrapped around me.

"Does a dragon's mate become a dragon too?"

"No. Her lifespan will match his, though, and her body changes. She becomes faster and stronger than a human. Like a dragon in his human form." I gritted the words out. *"Tighter."*

She gripped me harder. "Like that?"

I couldn't suppress my low growl. "Yes."

"You want more?"

"Fuck, yes."

She laughed. "Tell me what else I don't know about mating."

The woman had complete power over me, and she knew it. Maybe it should've pissed me off, but I was proud of her for taking control.

And I was already getting far more than I'd hoped she would offer.

"Heat doesn't only start the first time you meet a compatible human—it can start at any point. After a deep conversation. A shared smile. A joke. A glare. A fight. Unmated dragons don't connect with humans in any way, because it's too much of a risk. Can't connect with other supernaturals either, because we have to be neutral."

Her hand tightened around my erection.

I had to clench my jaw to stop myself from losing control. Had to close my eyes, too. She looked too damn good.

"So you've never had sex before?"

"No."

"Has anyone ever touched you like this before?"

"You're the first, Fireball."

"Well, that's hot," she said.

She dragged her hand slowly down my length, and I nearly lost it then and there.

"Can dragon guys have multiple orgasms?"

All supernatural guys could.

I couldn't let myself consider why she knew to ask that, though. Not if she wasn't going to let me hunt Dickwad down and remove his head from his body.

At least Bash had let me know he was dealing with the vampire situation. Elodie had given Brynn her ex's name, so I had to trust my sister's mate to take care of it.

"Yes."

"Then why are you holding back, August?"

"This is your show, remember?" My voice was still strained.

She smiled. "What else don't I know?"

"I'll be fighting the urge to bite you, soon. My bite gives you some of my magic, and my scent. It won't hurt."

"Sounds sexy." She stroked me again, and I snarled, too close to the edge.

"Mated dragons are codependent. If we sealed the bond, you'd go into heat every month. It would only last a day or two, but it would be excruciating if I didn't fuck you through it. The magic would form a mental connection between us, too. We could communicate with our minds, no matter how far apart we were. For now, we can only do so while I'm in my dragon form."

"But we'd never be far apart, right? Because you couldn't fly without me?" she continued working my cock.

"Right. A dragon would never let his wings walk away from him for long."

"Anything else?"

"I can't fucking think anymore, Fireball."

"Step closer, then."

I didn't hesitate to do so.

She sucked in a breath when my chest met hers, her soft breasts pressed against my thick muscles. I slipped my fingers into her hair, the way I'd wanted to since I saw the soft, wild strands.

"You did it again," I growled. "The thing where you breathed in."

"Because I'm attracted to you. Get over it, August."

"Don't think I can ever get over *that*."

Her perfect body was pressed against mine as she stroked my cock, and it was too much.

I snarled, driving into her fist as I lost control. Her fingers dug into my shoulder as I moved against her, and she was breathing almost as fast as I was when my climax ended.

Her cheeks were flushed.

The smell of her desire was thick, despite the water falling behind me.

She wanted me.

I was still hard, and aching for her.

"Open your thighs and let me see how you touch yourself," I ordered, chest rising and falling harshly.

I needed to watch her unravel like I needed to breathe.

Her face flushed, but she parted her legs.

I released her hair and sank to my knees, leveling my gaze with her hot, slick core.

Her expression grew a little self-conscious, and she started closing her legs again—but I caught her knees, holding them where they were. "You're the sexiest thing I've ever seen, Fireball. Don't hide from me."

Her face was red, but she dipped her head, opening herself wider.

Her fingers slid through her folds, and I watched hungrily as she circled the ridge that must've been her clit.

Her touch was slow, but not soft.

Smooth, but not gentle.

I tried like hell to hold back, but she smelled too good.

My hand caught hers, our fingers intertwining as my mouth found her core.

She gasped, her free hand finding my hair and tangling in the strands.

I focused on her clit, mimicking her motions, trying like hell not to lose myself to the taste of her.

She was so fucking delicious.

I *devoured* her.

She cried out with her climax once, her body jerking and her face twisting in ecstasy.

Her cries were louder with the second, my tongue working her harder and faster.

And with the third, my mate screamed her pleasure for me. I shattered with her, my hand on my cock as her taste sent me over the edge.

She pushed my face away from her core weakly, her expression dazed. The back of her head rested against the wall, and her legs were shaking so much, I didn't dare let go.

"Well, you're a fast learner," she managed. "Can't say I expected that."

My chest rumbled. "I could eat you all day, Fireball."

She dragged her fingers through my hair. "I don't think I'm ready for that."

Maybe not, but she would be before the heat was over.

And I'd never get enough of it. Not to last me through the rest of my immortal life.

I barely knew her, but I already knew that walking away from her was going to hurt like hell.

eight
ELODIE

OUR, uh, *shower* erased whatever awkwardness had remained between us after our talk on the porch.

There was no more discomfort.

No more uncertainty.

We were stuck together for four weeks in the cabin, and we were going to make the most of it.

...And finish my classes, of course. I had to do that too.

August walked with me to my room, and sat on the edge of my bed with a towel wrapped around his waist. He watched me dig through my laundry basket, then get dressed.

Wearing a lot of clothing was a no go, because we needed so much physical contact to appease the magic. So, I pulled on a pair of tight spandex shorts, and a simple black bralette. It wasn't cute, but it was comfortable.

His gaze was almost predatory as he watched me get dressed. "I'm putting my shirt on you again before you see my brother."

"Probably a good call. Wouldn't want you to have to kill him."

His eyes burned hotter.

The man was insatiable. How was he still horny after what we'd done in the shower? I might not be able to walk after the next four weeks.

At least I'd go out with a bang.

Literally.

"Eli's probably outside now. He and Gordon know better than to come up to the porch," August said, as I stepped up to him and put my hands on his shoulders. His hands slid up the backs of my thighs, and he pulled me closer. "I'll check."

"After you put pants on?"

He chuckled. "You already want me covered, Fireball?"

"I do have work to get done. All this is a little distracting." I gestured to his chest.

"Guess I better wear a shirt, then."

"Guess so."

He slid his hands up my ass, squeezing. "How much do I get to touch you today?"

My face warmed. "Depends how much work I get done."

"We'd better get going, then." He finally stood, not releasing my backside until the very last second.

We made a quick stop in the bathroom, so I could tie my hair up in a tangled bun, before making it to his room. There, August got dressed, then tugged one of his shirts over my head, as promised.

I once again tried to inhale his scent off the fabric, but barely smelled anything. "Would my sense of smell get better if we sealed the bond?"

He nodded. "Not as good as mine, but it would improve significantly. You'll be able to tell the difference after I bite you."

Considering I'd dated a vampire, the biting thing wasn't weird to think about. He'd bitten me many times, and it always felt good. I didn't see why it wouldn't be similar with August.

Our arms brushed as we headed out to the porch. I let myself overthink it for a few second, biting my lip hard, before I finally slipped my hand into August's. He squeezed it lightly, so I laced my fingers between his.

When his chest rumbled in satisfaction, I fought a smile.

It felt nice.

Really, really nice.

And not just because it kept the heat and pain at bay. His

hand was strong and warm, and something about it felt right.

Okay, maybe it was just the bond.

I was alright with that, though.

We made it outside, and sure enough, Eli and Gordon had dragged some of the porch furniture out to the dirt in front of the cabin. Not my favorite swing, thankfully. I'd learned enough about August to know that my ass wasn't going anywhere near a chair that smelled like his brother.

Eli flashed us a lazy grin. There was a wicked glint in his eyes.

August spoke first. "Forget whatever you're about to say, asshole."

Eli laughed, loudly.

Gordon smirked.

It still seemed safe to assume Eli was the fun one out of the three Sky brothers.

"Good to know you haven't lost your mind yet, Auggie," Eli said.

"You know I'll tell you if that starts," August grumbled.

"He's treating you well, El?" Eli asked, finally looking at me. Unlike his brother, he didn't stare or mentally strip me down. His attention was respectful.

"You must've talked to Brynn," I said.

"Yup. She made us dinner. She loves you, by the way."

"I like her too. And August's a perfect gentleman." I patted his bicep with my free hand, since the other was still tangled with his. "We're just peachy."

Eli's grin grew wicked again, and August snapped at him. "Shut it."

"I didn't say anything."

"Your face said enough."

I bit my lip to hide a smile.

I kind of loved seeing them interact like that. Like normal people, normal siblings.

"Your *scent* says en—"

"We're going back inside. I'm sane. Fuck off," August growled.

Eli laughed as August tucked me in front of him and walked me back to the porch. His chest brushed my back as we went, and it felt nice.

Really nice.

He shut the door behind us, and let out a long breath. "Sorry."

"Don't apologize. No one died, so that makes it a win, right?"

His eyes softened, his lips curving grudgingly. "Sure, Fireball."

I smiled. "Can you help me move the porch swing to the other side of the cabin? I want to work outside, but I don't think you want me facing your brother while I do."

"You think correctly." He squeezed my hand lightly before releasing it. "And I've got it."

"Thanks."

He stepped back outside, and I heard his heavy footsteps moving around the porch. I grabbed my laptop, and met him at the back door as he pushed the porch swing easily into its new place.

"How strong are you?" I asked, curiosity taking hold again.

He shrugged. "Strong enough."

I guess it made sense that he wouldn't have lifted weights or anything to figure out exactly how much he could carry. He hadn't struggled with the gigantic, awkwardly-large porch swing, though. So he obviously wasn't weak.

His side met mine as he sat down, and my shoulders relaxed as heat and soreness I'd barely noticed vanished quickly.

"I'm going to send Eli and Gordon to your university. Is there any information the school will need? An ID number or something?"

Oh.

Right.

At least he was still thinking about things like that, because I obviously wasn't.

I gave him my student ID number and full name, and he wrote them down before going over to talk with his brother.

Warmth and soreness started to set in again as soon as he was gone, but he made it back pretty quickly and sat down beside me. There was a phone in his hand when he did—it looked brand new, and didn't have a case on it.

"Did Eli give you that?" I asked.

"Yup. We leave our Scale Ridge phones at Brynn's place. Our normal phones are at the mountain. We don't try to haul them with us when we fly back and forth."

"Mate Mountain?"

"Some humans and supernaturals call it that. To us, it's just home."

I liked that. "Do you miss the mountains while you're here?"

"Yes and no. Since my parents died, I've spent more time in Scale Ridge than back at home. And when I'm there, I've been dealing with the thunder being assholes."

"And now Jasper took over?"

"Yes. Finally."

I laughed. "After your six months in prison, are you going to stay at the mountain?"

"I'm undecided on that." He lifted a shoulder. "Tradition says I need to rejoin the rotation guarding the prison as soon as I'm free. My gut brings me back here."

"But when you're here, you're constantly worried about sending someone into heat?"

He nodded.

"And that won't change when our bond is broken?"

"Not that I know of. An unmated shifter is an unmated shifter. We have no control over our magic when it comes to heat."

"Wow. You could walk away from this when it's over and send another woman into heat the next day," I said, gesturing between us.

I wasn't sure how I felt about that.

Irritated, maybe?

Like an object?

There was nothing special about me to him. I was just the unfortunate woman whose scent he caught at the worst possible time.

"Theoretically. In practice, it doesn't work that way. Hardly anyone makes it through without sealing the bond, remember? The only couple I know of that did ended up as mates shortly after heat ended anyway."

He *had* told me that.

We were just going to have to be the outliers.

"If it had happened, that dragon would immediately be questioned," August added. "His tactics would be incorporated throughout the world, and he'd probably brag about it. It wouldn't be a secret."

"But we're not becoming mates."

"We can't," he agreed. "And for the record, I've unintentionally come face to face with an assload of human women over the years. I raised Brynn here, which meant taking her to school, dance, and the grocery store, on top of everything else. I had to accept that taking a mate would probably happen when I moved with her to Scale Ridge when she was an infant."

"But it never did?"

He shook his head. "None of their scents caught my attention. Yours did, immediately. That's not insignificant."

So there *was* something special about me to him. And he wanted me to understand that.

We just couldn't do anything about it, even if we wanted to.

Which we didn't.

So... yeah.

That was it.

"Why did you raise her?" I asked.

"Our parents died. There were complications when our mother gave birth to her, and our parents lives were tied together with a mate bond, so they both passed on. Traditionally, a mated couple takes a parentless female infant to a human city to raise her, but on their deathbed, they asked us to do it. They didn't want her growing up with strangers, or even with friends. They wanted us to be her family."

My throat closed.

That was really, really sad.

"So when they passed, we inherited the throne and an infant. It was a struggle. Though I was technically the head of the thunder, Jasper was much better at keeping the peace, so he had to stay in the mountains most of the time when Brynn was young. Eli had already been running the prison's guard rotations, so he kept that mantle. For the first few years, I was about all she had. Things eased up after that, and the thunder grew insistent that I show my face more often, so we split our time with her almost equally to appease them."

"Why did they want to see you?"

"They didn't agree with us raising her. Like I said, dragons are very traditional. I'm not, but most of the others are. There's a dragon in our prison right now who was put away by his own thunder for murdering a small, influential clan of vampires who had hurt his sister. I would've done the same thing. The only reason my sentence is six months, instead of a lifetime, is because the Villins did the dirty work for me when Brynn's life was in danger."

"The Villins?"

"Bash's family. Their last name is Villin."

Huh.

What an unfortunate last name.

Then again, August's was *Sky*.

August Sky.

Not any better than Bash Villin.

"Sounds like you don't really belong with the thunder," I said.

"Not really. Somehow, they're still my family, though. If anything goes wrong, I know they'll have my back."

Our conversation trailed off, and I returned to the project I was working on.

After a few minutes, August's foot began to tap on the ground. It distracted me, but only a little.

When the tapping grew louder, I sighed.

He stopped.

After a moment of silence, he asked, "Can I rub your feet? I'm losing my mind just sitting here."

I blinked.

Could he *what*?

All women in existence knew a *foot rub* was a code for sex.

He had a phone, so he could just watch a movie or something if he was bored.

"I have to work on this," I said, gesturing to my laptop.

His forehead creased. "I assumed you would keep working."

"I know that's code for sex, August."

His forehead creased further. "What?"

"Didn't you ever watch TV when you were raising Brynn?"

"Kid shows, sometimes."

Maybe he really did just want to rub my feet.

"If I was trying to seduce you, I wouldn't need your feet to do it," he said. "I just have the urge to touch you. If you don't want me to, I won't."

Oh.

Well, when he put it like that...

I scooted to the far side of the swing, adjusting the pillows before I lifted my feet onto his lap. "They're all yours."

His lips curved upward, just a little. "Now you're speaking my language."

I laughed. "I think I like you, *Auggie*."

Eli had used the nickname to bother him, but I thought it was fun.

"I think I like you too, *Fireball*."

He started rubbing my feet, and I fought a groan.

Maybe there was a reason *foot rub* translated to *sex*.

IT TOOK me a few minutes to adjust to the glorious feeling of his hands working my feet before I managed to focus on my work again. But, I eventually got sucked back into my project.

The next few hours passed quickly, and soon enough, August was stepping away to make lunch. I missed his touch immediately, but survived the few minutes apart with minimal pain and sweating. When he came back with peanut butter and banana sandwiches, I murmured my thanks and kept working, taking bites when he nudged my feet to remind me to eat.

After we were done, I went back to work.

And he went back to massaging me.

It was the most I'd ever enjoyed schoolwork in my life.

nine

ELODIE

IT WAS late in the afternoon when August finally released my feet again and told me he needed to make dinner. My brain felt a little mushy, so I closed my laptop and left it on the swing, following him into the kitchen.

He cooked by memory, so I followed his instructions, working with him so we could stay together. Though the main purpose was to avoid the pain and sweatiness that would accompany heat, I liked cooking with him.

It was kind of relaxing.

And for a few minutes, I let myself believe that the way he constantly sought me out, touching my hips, arms, and face every chance he had, was just because he liked doing so.

I knew it wasn't true, but it made me feel nice to believe it anyway.

And I was still wearing his shirt, so it wasn't like I looked really hot or seductive.

When we sat down to eat together, his bare feet brushed mine. It was to keep the heat at bay—but I liked it.

We ate in comfortable silence for a few minutes before I asked, "Are you going to let me see you in your dragon form?"

He studied me before he answered. "What will you give me in exchange?"

"What do you want?"

There was another moment of silence before he said, "A kiss."

"How much of a kiss?"

His chest rumbled. "As much as you'll give me."

"Have you ever kissed anyone before?"

"Not the way you're referring to."

He'd probably kissed his baby sister on the cheek before or something.

And he'd technically kissed *me*. Just not on the lips.

My face reddened at the reminder.

It wasn't like making out was any more intimate than what we'd already done. And since we had four weeks to enjoy ourselves... well, we might as well have fun.

"Deal."

His gaze grew hungry as he watched me eat, apparently no longer caring about his food.

When I was finished, I abandoned my plate, stepping over to where he sat at the table.

August started to stand—but I put my hand to the center of his chest and pushed him back down.

His hands found my hips as I lowered myself onto his lap, his erection hard against my center. That warmed me too, but in a way I liked.

"Anything I should know first?" he asked, his gaze on my mouth.

"Just follow your instincts and have fun." I slipped my hands into his hair, tipping his head as I leaned in and pressed my lips to his.

He was stiff at first, his mouth not moving at all.

But when I found the seam of his lips, he parted without hesitation.

His growl rumbled against my chest at the first brush of my tongue on his.

His hands tightened on my hips with the second.

And with the third, he finally kissed me back.

He was tentative at first.

Slow.

Sweet.

Sensual.

But he adapted quickly, and the kiss went from simmering to burning in what felt like a heartbeat.

His hands found my ass, and pulled me down over his erection a little harder.

Mine moved over his neck and to his arms, gripping his thick biceps like anchors.

We kissed, and kissed, and kissed until I finally pulled away.

My chest rose and fell rapidly, but I released one of his arms. "If you want more, you have to take me flying."

His eyes blazed. "You drive me mad, Fireball."

I smiled.

August carried me out of the house without another word.

ELI AND GORDON were still outside, kicking back in their chairs, but August ignored them.

I waved, not wanting them to be offended.

Eli waved back, but Gordon just glared.

"Gordon seems like a jerk sometimes," I whispered to August.

He snorted. "He is one. And he's going to follow us the whole time we're in the sky, to make sure I don't run away."

"You wouldn't do that." I wasn't sure why I felt so confident about it, but I did.

"Nope." He let go of my hand, and peeled his shirt over his head.

I bit my lip as he unbuttoned his jeans, stepping out of them smoothly. His boxer-briefs followed.

"Step back, Fireball." The command was smooth, not even slightly harsh.

I moved away, giving him more space.

August took a deep breath in, and his golden skin shimmered as he let it out. With his second inhale, his body changed. And with his second exhale, he stretched his scaled neck to the sky, loosing a small stream of fire.

Though I'd known dragon shifters existed, and seen pictures of them before, I couldn't help but be awestruck by the sight of him.

He was massive.

Strong.

Elegant.

Powerful.

His deep silver scales glittered in the setting sun, the strong lines of his elegant body sharpened by the light filtering around them.

He was stunning.

August took a step toward me, lowering his head until we were eye-to-eye.

I sucked in a breath when he leaned forward.

And let it out with a laugh when he licked my cheek.

He lowered his belly to the ground, then set his head down right in front of me. I crouched, reaching for his nose with a questioning look.

August closed his eyes, giving me permission, and I closed the rest of the distance. My palm landed on his warm, smooth scales. There was something about them that felt sort of soft. Not like fur, or hair, but something else. I couldn't put my finger on it, but they were comfortable.

He licked the underside of my arm, and a laugh escaped me.

His chest rumbled, the sound happy.

I smiled.

"Fly with me, Fireball." His voice was in my mind, catching me off-guard. He had mentioned mental communication while he was in his dragon form, but I hadn't really considered what it would sound or feel like.

"Are you sure?" I asked my question aloud, not certain if I could speak into his mind too.

And not sure he'd want me to, even if I could.

"I'm always sure."

"Okay. Don't let me fall, though."

He narrowed his beastly eyes at me. *"I'm going to pretend you didn't just say that."*

I huffed out a laugh.

He was a pain in the ass, but I liked it for some reason.

I stood up and walked around to his side, eyeing the distance between the ground and the back of his neck. It was at least four feet high. "I think I need a stepstool."

He snorted.

"Need a lift, El?" Eli called from across the yard.

August growled.

"Nah," I yelled back. "Don't want to smell like you. Thanks though."

"You've got it."

I didn't know if I did, but it was time to find out.

Stepping up to his side, I ran my hand down the smooth length of his scales.

Wow, I loved how he felt.

He hummed at my touch, so he must've enjoyed it.

Finally, I set my hands on the back of his neck and went up on my tiptoes. In one motion, I pulled up and threw my leg over him.

My knee smashed into his side before I crashed back to the ground, landing on my ass.

August made a coughing sound, and I laughed hard.

Yeah, that was a fail.

Eli and Gordon were both choking back laughter when I looked over at them, still on my butt.

"Dad used his tail to lift mom up," Eli hollered. "Try that."

"Hmm." August's voice was considerate. *"I do remember that."*

"You just wanted to see me land on my butt," I teased, brushing off my backside as I stood up.

He laughed into my mind. *"I prefer staring at your ass when it's not covered in dirt, actually."*

"Probably true." I stepped up to his side again, and his thick tail curved around my side.

"Definitely true. Drape your arms over the top of my tail."

I lifted my arms over the spiky, scaled appendage. In a slow, smooth motion, he lifted me off my feet and up to the place where his neck met his shoulders.

I leaned up against his neck, and he made a satisfied noise as he pulled his tail away from me. *"There we go. Comfortable?"*

"I guess."

He chuckled into my mind. *"Arms around me."*

"You swear you're not going to let me fall?"

"I swear. Even if you did fall, I would catch you."

"What?!"

"Just hold on, Fireball."

With that, he took off.

We shot into the sky. My arms and legs clamped down on his scales as wind whipped against me, terror holding me tightly.

"Breathe," August commanded.

Breathing *was* necessary.

I just couldn't manage to make it happen.

"We'll level out in a second. I'm not letting you pass out, El. Breathe, now." His order was so authoritative, I found myself taking in a deep breath.

The air was colder, and fresher.

My hold on August didn't loosen, but I did keep breathing.

We finished ascending, and as he'd promised, began gliding.

My eyes widened as I took in the mountains not above us, but around us.

Below us.

My breath caught in my throat for an entirely different reason.

It was stunning.

Gorgeous, untouched land.

The wind rushing against us.

The world silent around me.

"Wow," I whispered.

The word never met my ears, lost in the wild around me.

That was the only name for it.

Wilderness.

Pure, undisturbed wilderness.

And flying on August's back, I felt like I was a part of it.

I never would've expected to like it, but I did.

I loved it.

"Still breathing?" August asked me. Since he'd noticed when I stopped, I was pretty sure he already knew the answer. So, he just wanted to talk.

I couldn't yell over the sound of rushing wind. Instead, I focused on the way it felt when he spoke into my mind, then spoke back. *"Now that we're not ascending, yes."*

"What do you think?"

"Of flying? It's incredible." My voice was soft, but genuine. *"Terrifying at first, though."*

"You'll get used to it."

"You plan on taking me flying often, Auggie?"

He chuckled. *"Yes."*

We only had four weeks. We'd have to be in the sky every other or third day to really fly *often* before the bond broke, unless he was referring to us flying together after he got out of prison.

And I knew he wasn't doing that.

So, I changed the subject.

"Bet this is how you woo all your women." My voice was playful.

"Of course. Might as well use my best asset."

"I don't know, you have some pretty good assets..."

He laughed into my mind.

The sound was light and free. Peaceful. Content.

My smile lingered as I leaned against his neck a little more, my grip loosening slightly.

Maybe heat wasn't such a bad thing after all.

Maybe I could enjoy it in even more ways than I'd thought.

ten

AUGUST

FLYING with Elodie was different than flying on my own.

I loved flying.

But flying with her...

It was better.

Happier, too.

Her body was warm against my scales, the gentle weight of her somehow steadying me.

She belonged there with me.

In the sky.

On my back.

With me.

I barely knew her, but I'd already started to realize that it was going to hurt like hell to walk away from her.

If I could walk away from her at all.

I'd met my mate...

And she was mine.

End of the discussion.

I'd started to see why mated dragons didn't fly without their females, too.

Because what was the point?

Why take to the sky alone when you could enjoy it so much more with your companion?

My thoughts continued to move as we glided over the mountains. Though I was headed toward Mate Mountain, I wouldn't take her there.

Not when the bastards in the thunder would only try to turn her against me.

Or when they might look at her, speak with her, smell her...

No.

She was mine.

And I was going to hold her tightly, for as long as I could.

eleven

ELODIE

IT WAS LATE AT NIGHT—OR early in the morning —when we finally got back to the cabin. I was still grinning when we stumbled into bed, and fell asleep with that stupid smile on my face.

The sun was shining through the windows way too brightly when I finally woke up.

My face felt glued to August's bare chest with sweat, and his hand was gliding over my back slowly. Though I was still wearing his big t-shirt, he'd slipped his hand underneath it, so his skin was on mine.

"You can unbuckle my bra if you want," I mumbled against his chest.

He rumbled lightly against me, and undid it without a moment's pause.

My body heated further as he dragged his hand over my skin again.

"Good morning, Fireball."

"Good morning." My voice was soft, my face even warmer than the rest of me.

"How are you feeling?"

"Hot."

He chuckled. "You *are* hot."

I got the feeling he wasn't talking about my temperature. "So are you."

"There *is* fire burning in my veins."

"Pretty sure it's burning in mine for now."

"Most of it." The tips of his short fingernails dragged over my back, and a soft groan escaped me at the blissfulness of it.

His erection throbbed below my hip.

My stomach growled loudly, and he chuckled again. "Guess I need to feed you."

"Guess so." I was a little disappointed at the interruption.

Mostly because I'd been hoping we would have a repeat of our experience in the shower.

But if August was to be believed, there would be *plenty* of that in the coming weeks.

...Pun still not intended.

So, eating was only a temporary interruption.

He brushed a kiss to my forehead before slipping out from beneath me to use the bathroom. The heat that washed over me at his absence was more intense than it had been the day before, and the soreness was worse too.

I wasn't sure what to think of that.

Or whether to worry about how much worse that soreness was going to get.

August's hands brushed my shoulder as he passed me on the way to the kitchen, giving me a moment of relief.

I made my way into the bathroom, snorting when I saw my hair.

It was an utter trainwreck.

Dry and knotted, with tangles I worried might rip right out of my hair if I didn't soak them in conditioner first. Between the shitty four-in-one soap and the hours of flying, it had seen much better days.

My hair was finicky. When it got bad, it took ages to get it back to normal.

So, I needed to call my mom and ask about that unscented shampoo ASAP.

But that phone call was going to lead to her panicking and questioning my sanity.

There wasn't a good alternative, though.

I'd do it after breakfast, I decided.

I HELPED August make bacon and eggs, then cleaned up with him. Something hit our door as we finished, and August grumbled about his brother on his way to answer it.

When he tugged it open, Eli called out, "Daily sanity check."

August looked back at me.

I waved him out the door. "I'm fine. Go chat with him. I have to call my mom anyway."

"I'll make it quick."

He stepped outside, leaving the door open as he headed out.

I slipped into my assigned bedroom, even though I had yet to really sleep in it.

I ignored heat's side effects as I shut myself inside. The door stayed unlocked, in case the pain got too bad and I needed August.

Hitting the button to video call my mother, I braced myself for her discomfort.

She answered immediately. "Hey, Elodie!"

Before I could echo her greeting, her face crinkled. There was suspicion in her gaze that grew deeper as she took me in.

"Where are you?" she asked.

"It's a long story."

She waited.

I sighed.

"Elodie."

"Alright, fine. I met a dragon shifter."

Her eyebrows lifted.

"I guess we're soulmates." I tried to remember all of the BS August had spewed to my friends when he gave them the closest explanation to the truth that he could manage. "Maybe. Potentially soulmates. We're stuck together for the next few weeks as we wait for the bond to either break or become permanent."

Her eyebrows shot higher. "Tell me you're kidding."

"I think I know better than to kid about supernaturals at this point, mom."

Her shock slowly faded to a pinched, uncertain worry. "What exactly does this consist of?"

"He took me flying yesterday. On his back, in the sky. It was incredible," I admitted. "The wind in my hair, the mountains below us... I've never done anything like it."

"That's great, but you know it isn't what I'm talking about."

"I know." I tucked my hair behind my ear. "I'm living with him. In his cabin, in the woods. It's beautiful here, and he's very respectful. He didn't want this any more than I did, but we're dealing with it as well as we can."

"His name?"

"August."

"I want to meet him."

"Mom," I protested. "I—"

The bedroom door opened, and August came striding in. He didn't remark on my choice of bedroom, but came over to sit down beside me. He put his hand on my thigh to give me relief from heat's effect, and I reluctantly handed him the phone.

He held it in front of him like he'd done so a hundred times. "Hello, Mrs. Jacobs."

His voice was respectful, and his expression was a pleasant neutral.

"You're a dragon?" my mom didn't beat around the bush.

"I am. I'm sure you can see the fire in my eyes right now. It's a product of our potential mate bond."

My mom nodded, though she did so reluctantly.

"The mating process is always chaperoned among dragons, so my brother and another male shifter are outside the house right now. I can show you where they are, if it would comfort you."

"It would."

August stood again, squeezing my thigh before he strode away.

He was back a few moments later, said goodbye to my mom, and gave me back my phone.

She looked slightly less worried when she was on the screen again.

"So, not to change the subject, but I need to try some kind of unscented shampoo and conditioner. I guess shifters have sensitive noses."

Her worry gave way to interest all of the sudden.

She loved talking about hair products.

"I've heard that. Marissa has some shifter clients. Give me a few minutes to call around and find out what they're using, and I'll get back to you."

I agreed, and we said quick goodbyes before she hung up.

August came back in the room as soon as I turned it off, taking a seat beside me and draping an arm over my shoulder. I leaned against him, and he squeezed my arm lightly.

"How's she feeling about it?"

"Seems okay now. She was upset at first, but I think she's getting over it. The hair thing gives her something else to worry about."

"Good." He kissed my forehead lightly. So lightly, I wondered if I'd imagined it. "You're handling it well."

"I like to think so."

"I'm not wondering, Fireball. You're dealing with it better than I would've expected. Better than I am, too."

I rolled my eyes. "You're cool, calm, and collected all the time."

He snorted. "I'm a warm, angry mess."

"You are not."

"Sure I am. Can't even get the sight of you in the shower out of my head or mouth."

"You're still tasting me?"

"In my dreams. Including daydreams. And those dreams are *constant*."

"We can make that a reality."

"Can we?" His hand dragged over my thigh, lightly.

"Mmhm."

"How?"

He wanted me to tell him exactly what I needed him to do to me.

My face was flushed. "Start with taking my shorts off."

I was still wearing the spandex from the night before.

His fingers were slightly rough against my skin as he slipped the tips of them under the waistband, then slowly peeled them down my thighs.

His chest was rumbling in satisfaction when my legs were free, my lower half exposed to the world.

Well, not the world.

Just August.

"You smell so fucking good."

The words made my toes curl, and he hadn't even touched me yet.

"My shirt, too," I breathed.

"*My* shirt, you mean?"

"No, you made it mine when you forced me to wear it."

He peeled it over my head. "Excuse me—*your* shirt."

A soft laugh escaped me. "Thank you."

"Any time, Fireball."

My shirt hit the floor, and his hands found my breasts. I'd left my bra in the bathroom after I used the facilities. He'd already unbuckled it for me, so there hadn't been a point in refastening it.

"Damn." His voice was nearly feral. "I love you naked."

"You're not so bad yourself." I dragged my fingers lightly down the dips and ridges of his thick, strong abdomen.

He was gorgeous. Absolutely gorgeous.

I didn't think I could ever get enough of him.

When I found the button on his shorts, he swore as I undid it.

And cursed again when I pushed the waistband down, freeing his erection.

My hand wrapped around his length, and his lips twisted in a silent snarl.

Before I could have my way with him, he rolled me smoothly to my stomach, lifted me up to my hands and knees, and positioned himself beneath me.

The back of his head was on the bed.

I was sitting on his face.

My moan was automatic when he tongued my clit. My body's movements were too.

I rocked.

I bobbed.

I jerked.

And soon enough, I was crying out on his mouth as I unraveled.

His chest rumbled the whole time, the scratch of his stubble on my legs and lady bits as he ate me out. I didn't mind the burn when I was enjoying myself so much.

My phone rang—and August slowed down.

"I'll call her back," I breathed.

"She'll worry," he growled against me.

I couldn't stop my hips from moving again, but his hands clamped down on my thighs.

"Answer the damn call if you want more, Fireball."

My hand shook a little as I unburied the device from the blankets.

My face in the camera looked a tiny bit flushed, but otherwise normal. It was fine. I'd be fine.

August threw the blankets up over my shoulders without climbing out from under me, so I caught them and tugged them into place. I finished covering myself and hit the button just in time to stop it from going to the voicemail graveyard. I never checked voicemail. Did *anyone* check voicemail?

"Hey, mom."

"Hey!" Her eyes were bright. She must've had fun researching unscented shampoo and conditioner. "I talked to a handful of the stylists I work with and came up with a list of options. After I compared them all, I realized there were three that have the best chance of working out for you. So, I ordered you a set of each of them. You should be able to pick them up at the nearest beauty store within an hour or so. Just show them your ID when you get there. They technically aren't supposed to sell to you, but I spoke to them on the phone and convinced them it was fine."

She would've definitely tracked my location to see where I was before calling me, and before ordering for me.

"Perfect. Thanks, mom." My voice still didn't sound exactly right, but she didn't notice, thankfully.

"Of course. Facetime me again after you try each of them so we can compare."

A soft laugh escaped me. "Alright."

She smiled. "Love you, honey."

"Love you too." I hung up, and August's tongue dragged over my clit.

A cry escaped me, and my hips jerked hard.

"Turn the volume off on that thing, Fireball. No more interruptions."

I shut the volume off, and dropped it on the bed.

He sucked my clit between his teeth, and I cried out, hips bucking and hands diving into his hair.

I wanted more.

I needed more.

"Give me your fingers," I commanded.

He dragged one over my entrance, and I nearly climaxed at the feel of it alone. "You like that?" he spoke against my core, making me crazy.

"I need it inside me."

The fire in his eyes burned brighter. "You need my cock."

"Yes. But your fingers will have to be enough."

He pressed harder against my entrance when he found it again—then slid his finger inside me.

I sucked in a breath as it entered me, my body clenching tightly around it.

It wasn't big enough.

It wasn't what I wanted.

But I'd have to deal with that.

"More?" His gaze was hot.

Fierce.

Claiming.

"Always."

The fire in his eyes grew again, and he added a second finger.

That felt better.

When he added a third, my hips were finally moving the way they wanted to. His tongue was doing what I wanted, too. And his body...

I loved having his body beneath mine.

His face under me.

On me.

Devouring me.

"Come for me, Fireball." The order was low.

Filthy.

And exactly what I wanted to hear.

I cried out, rocking my hips until his fingers were hooked where I wanted them.

Until I was shattering, finding my pleasure once again on his hands and face.

It was everything.

Everything, and more.

EVENTUALLY, we made it out of the room. I'd touched him too, getting him off and giving him the relief he needed while he took me over the edge yet again.

I was still dazed as we climbed in a black SUV that I hadn't noticed in front of the cabin before. It was August's, and Eli had driven it over from Brynn's house for us at some point.

My car sat beside it, though mine was much older, smaller, and less shiny than August's.

And probably functioned worse, too.

Suffice it to say, when he led me to his vehicle instead of mine, I didn't argue.

Actually, I flashed him a small smile.

Which he returned.

Then, he kissed my forehead again—I knew I wasn't imagining that one—and walked around the car to find his seat.

His hand rested on my thigh as we drove away, left bare by the cutoff jean shorts and t-shirt I had on.

It might have been the most peaceful drive of my life.

twelve

ELODIE

WE PICKED up the shampoo and conditioner my mom had ordered without a problem. August's arm remained around me, and my defenses rose a little when I saw everyone in the shop drooling over him, but it was fine.

I survived.

When we got back to the cabin, I washed my hair, videoed my mom to show her the difference, then finally got out to the porch.

I spent the rest of the day working.

And August?

Well, he spent it rubbing my feet.

Not because he wanted sex. Because he liked touching me.

The man was spoiling me for everyone else.

But I didn't have the heart to ask him to stop. So, the spoiling commenced.

And it was blissful.

We made dinner together again, and went flying after we ate just like we had done the day before.

I enjoyed every single minute of it.

A FEW MORE DAYS PASSED BY the same way.

Food, sexy time, work, and flying, all on repeat. We shuffled the order sometimes, but they all had their moment in the sun.

We hadn't gone further than what we'd currently done, silently capping our sex life at him using his fingers and mouth while I only brought my hands to the table.

It was still incredible.

Even if I wanted more sometimes.

And ached to have actual penis-in-vagina sex.

My friends stopped by for a visit on the fourth or fifth day after the magic set in, but Randa and Vi didn't stay long. We chatted out in front of the cabin, and Randa and Eli flirted a bit, but heat's magic pushed me back to August's side pretty quickly. It was nice to see them, but the pain and warmth that accompanied distance from August was getting worse by the day.

. . .

A WEEK and a half had gone by when the heat stopped responding to August's touch.

I sat down at the kitchen table beside him, pressing the bottoms of my bare feet to the tops of his like always.

Before, it had given me relief from the warmth and pain.

But as I touched them to his, they did nothing for me.

My forehead wrinkled.

My lips curved downward.

I lifted my toes off the tops of his feet, and pressed them back down, trying again.

Still nothing.

If the pain eased at all, I didn't feel it.

My muscles had passed the aching stage earlier, and my pain became the stabbing kind. The hurt would come in waves, but it always came. And when it did, it was intense.

I sucked in a breath as it hit me hard for a moment.

Taking in air felt difficult.

My heart throbbed in my chest, seeming to clench as the pain deepened.

"You're hurting." The concern in August's voice was unmistakable. He was shirtless, like usual, wearing just a pair of boxers.

"I'm fine." I forced myself to try to sound chipper. It failed, but I'd figured it was worth a shot.

"Don't lie to me, Fireball. We're a team, remember?"

"Alright. Yes, I'm in pain. Putting my feet on yours isn't helping like it used to."

August's forehead knitted in concern. "The magic must be growing stronger."

"What does it want from us now?"

"After touching? Sex. Biting could buy us another few days. Maybe a week."

I nodded.

Biting still sounded hot, so I wasn't against it.

We'd get to it after breakfast.

I forced myself to take another bite of my food, trying hard to ignore the next wave of pain that was coming on—and the insane amount I was sweating. The bralette and spandex shorts I had on were damp, and not for a fun reason.

August's foot hooked one of the legs of my chair, and he dragged me closer.

I was struggling to chew and swallow the food in my mouth when his hands caught my waist—and lifted me onto his lap.

My mostly-bare back met his chiseled chest, and the intimate contact eased the pain just a little more.

"You're burning up." The concern in his voice made me feel good. Or at least, it made me *want* to feel good.

"I'm okay."

He ignored me, his hands gliding slowly over my abdomen and hips. More physical contact did help a little, but not enough to make the difference I wanted.

"Keep eating."

I sighed, but forced another bite into my mouth.

I knew from experience that August would get growly if I didn't eat enough. And while I liked him growly, he wouldn't take no for an answer if it got to that point, so arguing was useless.

His hands continued moving over my abdomen and hips while I forced a few more bites down. Heat's magic was intense enough that it was a huge struggle.

August's lips brushed the back of my neck as I took yet another bite.

I shivered in response.

He'd been doing that a lot—kissing the back of my neck.

I hadn't thought much about it. Most of my thoughts were occupied by my schoolwork and surviving heat.

When I managed to get that bite down, I nearly gagged.

My fork went down beside the plate.

I couldn't eat any more.

"You're alright, Fireball." August's voice was low, with an edge of a growl. "Put your hands on the table."

Though I didn't know why he'd given the instruction, I grabbed the edge of the wood.

His lips brushed the back of my neck once again—and I gasped when his teeth replaced them a heartbeat later.

A dragon's bite wasn't like a vampire's.

It wasn't pain, followed by lusty bliss.

It wasn't a bite to my jugular, searching for blood.

It was so much better.

His magic rolled through me, a wave of power.

Strength.

Freedom.

Energy.

An orgasm tore through me just like that, leaving me sucking in air as my body adjusted to the magic that mingled with the fire in my veins.

The power didn't feel like it belonged to me.

It felt like it was August's.

Like *I* was August's.

There was no pain from his bite—only pure, untainted belonging.

His magic was mine.

My body was his.

And that was exactly how it was supposed to be.

His chest was rumbling, almost purring, when he finally released my neck.

My breathing was still rapid, but my pain was entirely gone.

"Keep eating, Fireball." His command made goosebumps erupt on my arms.

His lips brushed the back of my neck again, and there was no pain where the wound should've been.

I finally picked up my fork with a trembling hand, and lifted another bite to my lips.

"You smell incredible." His hands were still moving over my abdomen.

I inhaled deeply at his words, and caught what must've been August's scent.

My lower belly tightened.

My toes curled.

I didn't have words to describe what he smelled like.

Trees?

Sex?

Freedom?

Some combination of those things, and more?

It was just like the scent I'd caught on his skin the day we first met, but so much more intense.

It didn't make sense, but every fiber of my being told me it was right for me. *He* was right for me.

His hands slid up to my breasts and squeezed lightly, distracting me from his scent. "I don't know how long this will relieve the pain."

"Some relief is better than none."

He made a noise of agreement, kissing the back of my neck again like he just couldn't help it. "My scent intertwines perfectly with yours."

"Does it?" I moved my hips a little, earning a growl as the motion caused friction between my ass and his erection.

A knock at the door interrupted us.

I sighed.

August grumbled.

When I started slipping off his lap to go answer it, he set me down on my feet. His arm went around my waist before we started walking, and he plucked one of his t-shirts off the couch on the way. It went over my head before August pulled the door open.

I blinked when we found Brynn on the porch.

Her scent hit me, and I couldn't stop my face from scrunching up. She smelled *wrong*.

Brynn smiled, looking between us. "How are you guys doing?"

Neither of us answered right away.

I was trying to breathe through my mouth, to avoid her scent mingling with August's, but it wasn't really working.

Curiosity filled her eyes.

My jaw clenched a little.

"We're fine," August finally said. "You brought cookies."

It wasn't a question, but there was a huge plate of cookies in her hands, so it didn't really need to be one.

"Yep!" She handed it over.

He took it.

"I think I'm interrupting something." She looked between us.

She could see lust, so she could probably guess what we'd been up to.

"You are. And your scent is clouding my mate's," August said. "Take a few steps back?"

"Right." She took multiple steps away.

"Does he still seem sane?" Eli yelled from the front yard, where his chair was still set up.

"Yep," she yelled back. "Possessive, though."

"As he should be."

August grumbled, and Brynn smiled. "I'll get out of your hair. I'm glad to see you're enjoying yourselves, though. I hope you like the cookies!"

She winked at us, then headed off.

August walked me backward a few steps, closing the front door as soon as we were far enough from it.

He set the plate of cookies on the floor.

Then, his lips found the back of my neck again.

I shivered at the intimate sensation of being kissed there. And there was still no pain.

"Did the bite heal already?"

"Yes. My bites will always heal immediately."

His hands moved slowly down the curve of my waist. "You were jealous, Fireball."

My palms met the door when he kissed the back of my neck again, then dragged his tongue slowly over the sensitive skin.

"Not *jealous*," I said.

"Oh, really?" He sounded amused.

And like he didn't believe me in the slightest.

I didn't really believe me either, so that made two of us.

"Mmhm. I was just... surprised."

"Surprised, huh?"

"Yep. Surprised by how she smelled."

"And how did she smell?"

"Not good."

"Why didn't she smell good?"

He had me with that one, and he knew it.

"I don't know, Auggie." I hoped the nickname would distract him from the question.

It didn't.

He stepped closer to me, until his erection was pressed against my lower back.

My cheek met the front door.

His hands slid under my shirt and up my abdomen, finding my breasts.

"Want me to tell you why she smelled bad, Fireball?"

He held the weight of my breasts, the smell of my desire thickening around us.

It was almost as strong as the scent of his.

"Go ahead."

His lips brushed my ear.

His thumbs teased my nipples.

My entire body tensed.

"Because I belong to you." He worked my nipples rougher.

Harder.

While he pressed me into the door.

"Do you?" I whispered.

"With everything I am."

Only for a few more weeks, but he didn't say that. So I wouldn't either.

Might as well enjoy the time we had together.

"Tell me you were jealous, Fireball." His command was low.

Hot.

"I was jealous." The admission escaped before I could even attempt to stop it. "Now that I can smell your scent, hers seemed wrong."

"Good." His hands released my breasts, sliding down my abdomen. One lingered on my hip, and the other slid between my thighs. "What do I smell like?"

"I don't know."

He gave me a disapproving growl.

"You don't smell like any*thing*. More like... feelings. Lust. Desire. Comfort. Belonging."

"That's better." He finally stroked me between my thighs, over my shorts.

"What do I smell like to you?"

"Mine." He touched me again. "Pleasure. Need. Home."

Well, that was intense.

He worked me with his fingers, and my mind left his words.

His hands were the only thing I could focus on.

I shattered, and shattered, and shattered.

And by the time we collapsed in bed together, I started to think maybe he smelled like home to me too.

thirteen

ELODIE

THE NEXT FEW days were peaceful.

It was strange to experience peace in the middle of heat's intense magic, but we did.

We spent hours and hours on the porch together. I made a ton of progress on my schoolwork, and he massaged my feet like he was being paid to do it.

He wasn't.

He just liked touching me.

Eli and Gordon had spoken with the school and gotten permission for me to finish everything as soon as I could, so I'd been working with my professors to wrap my classes up early. I needed to be done before we reached the worst of heat's magic.

They set up my finals online, so I made my way through the

last exams. The pain and warmth started slowly seeping back in, but it wasn't too bad.

My sense of smell didn't fade in the days that followed the bite. I found myself lifting the collar of my shirt—August's shirt—just to inhale his scent.

He always smelled amazing.

And when heat's magic got too difficult to deal with, we had no problem slipping into the bedroom together.

Or the shower.

Or the kitchen.

Or the living room.

I FINISHED my last final a week later.

It didn't feel as good as I'd expected it to.

It felt sort of... empty.

I blamed the feeling on heat so I didn't worry about it.

We celebrated with an afternoon of flying, finally getting back late at night. After we threw together a dinner of leftovers, we collapsed on the couch, and August turned on a movie.

We ate while it played. Though I was snuggled up in his arms, my entire body hurt.

I was coated in sweat.

Exhaustion had set in so deep, I could almost feel it in my bones.

"Your scent tells me you're hurting, Fireball." August's voice was gravelly. Though he still passed Eli's insanity checks every day, August was getting more animalistic each time. I didn't tell his brother that, but he had warned me repeatedly to let Eli know if I ever felt unsafe.

Even when he seemed animalistic, his focus was on making me feel good, so I wasn't anywhere near afraid of him.

"I'm surviving," I whispered.

It was an automatic answer.

The only one I could give without making him worry more. And despite us being a team, I didn't want him to worry. Not if there was nothing we could do about the pain.

He pulled me closer, his chest rumbling unhappily. "We talked about lying."

"I told you the truth. I'm surviving." My voice was raw. "At least I'm done with school."

"And you deserve a real celebration for that. More than I can give you." His fingers slipped into my soft waves, and he slid them through the loose strands slowly. When he reached the ends, he looped the length around his palm and lifted it to his nose.

Though my hair was slightly damp with sweat, his cock jerked against my back.

My lips curved slightly. "You give me plenty, Auggie." Though my voice was quiet, I hoped he could tell the words were genuine.

"Not enough."

"I'll go out with my friends to celebrate after this is over."

His grip on my hair tightened. Not enough to hurt—just enough to tell me how much he hated that idea. "Where?"

"There's a place in town that we like. Not one of the vampire clubs."

His chest rumbled fiercely. "Stay away from the blood-drinking bastards."

I'd told him how everything had progressed with Dickwad, so he knew what I'd been through for the most part.

We'd met at a vampire club after Randa dragged me and Vi there.

"I know." I closed my eyes, letting out a long breath. "I won't make that mistake again."

Every part of me ached.

I wanted a distraction, but I was tired of what we'd been doing. He touched me, or tasted me. I touched him.

We needed more.

I bit my lip when an idea came to me.

"Your scent changed." His growl was immediate.

"Mmhm." I bit my lip harder.

I wasn't sure how he would respond... but I wanted to find out.

"That smells like lust, Fireball."

"Can you let go of my hair?"

He slowly untangled his hand from the strands.

"And put your arms up along the back of the couch?"

He worked his jaw as he forced himself to let go of me, and do what I'd asked him to with his arms. I rarely took control when we were together—and he loved being in charge.

But maybe he'd let me have a turn.

I rolled over on his lap, easing myself down over him.

When I lifted my eyes to his, I found him staring at me.

The fire that had taken over those pretty blue eyes was *burning* for me.

He'd realized what I had planned.

My gaze followed the thick muscles of his arms down to his hands, and found them gripping the couch.

His abdomen was tensed, too.

He didn't move a muscle as I pulled his boxers down far enough to free his cock.

Or as lowered my lips to his hardness.

He choked on a curse when I wrapped them around his massive erection.

His hips jerked when I flicked my tongue against the underside of him.

He shook as he fought his desire when I bobbed over him, taking him deeper into my mouth.

My eyes lifted to his, and the ferocious intensity in his gaze nearly took my breath away. His jaw was clenched, and veins bulged on his neck and forehead.

He was struggling to stay in control.

To make the moment, and his pleasure, last.

I gripped his cock in my fist and released him for a moment, speaking against him. "That feel okay?"

He throbbed hard in my hand, grinding his teeth.

My lips curved upward, the bottom one still against his cock.

"If being inside you is even better than this, I don't know how I'm supposed to make it through heat without it." His voice was strained.

My smile curved wider. "After you finish in my mouth, I'll let you take over."

His eyes slammed shut.

His cock throbbed a few more times.

"You're unreal, Fireball."

"My specialty," I agreed, and wrapped my lips around him again.

He choked on his chuckle, and swore viciously.

His hips jerked roughly.

His abdomen tensed, and flexed.

I bobbed once, twice—and he snarled as he lost control.

The taste of his pleasure was incredible.

It made me hotter and wetter, but not because of the heat.

Because he tasted just as good as he smelled.

Eventually, his climax ended, and I opened my eyes.

His gaze was predatory.

Fiery.

Feral.

He reached out to my face and dragged his thumb slowly over a drop of his pleasure that had escaped through the corner of my mouth.

My body throbbed too.

I wanted him to touch me.

Needed him to touch me.

After he had the chance to take the control he craved so desperately.

August slid the bead over my top lip, coating me in more of him.

It was possessive.

Hot.

A declaration that I was his, at least for the moment.

His hands slid into my hair, taking the reins.

"You'll tell me if I'm too rough." It was a command, not a question.

I dipped my head slightly, and his grip on my hair tightened.

"You look perfect with my cock in your mouth, Fireball. You like the way I taste?"

I nodded again, and his grip tightened further.

"After this, I'm going to fuck you with my tongue while you blow me. Got it?"

I moaned around him.

His chest rumbled. "Good girl."

His hips rocked slightly, and he moved my head just a little, testing me. Seeing what I could handle.

It felt good to give him the lead again. To let him decide what he wanted, and how he wanted it. To be the one giving him pleasure, instead of the other way around.

And soon enough, we ended up positioned just like he promised.

My clit on his face. His cock in my mouth.

Both of us reaching new heights of ecstasy, as we fought like hell not to let ourselves give in to what we wanted even more:

Our bodies intertwined the way they were meant to be.

WE SPENT a few more days in bed and on the couch. We watched movies and made love with our hands and mouths, and it was amazing.

But the pain was getting worse.

I hurt constantly, only getting a break when we were actively bringing each other to climax.

Eating was a struggle.

Moving was a struggle.

August carried me everywhere he needed to go—mainly to the kitchen, to cook more things he could try to make me eat—and growled every time my scent changed to indicate I was in more pain.

He no longer passed Eli's sanity checks, but I'd told Eli to screw off when he asked me if I wanted him to get rid of his beastly brother.

August and I were a team, even when life was shitty.

And heat was being *really* shitty to me.

But I would survive.

I had to survive.

Neither of us could accept me going to jail, so survival was the only option.

I WOKE up in the middle of the night in so much pain, I couldn't rest.

I bit my cheek to keep myself from crying out, but the change in my scent dragged August from sleep as well. My back was to his chest, and we both had on underwear and nothing else. Though we wanted to sleep naked, we were both worried about what it could lead to.

"Where's the pain?" His voice was groggy but feral.

"Everywhere," I whimpered.

His body shook against mine as he fought his instincts.

The instincts I knew were screaming at him to strip me bare and fuck me hard.

He reached between my thighs, tearing my panties with the slightest of motions. When he pushed the fabric up my abdomen and opened my legs, I didn't protest.

I didn't *want* to protest.

I wanted him to take away my pain and fill me with his cock.

August draped one of my legs over his hips, holding me open for him, and slid three fingers inside me roughly.

The way I knew he wanted to take me.

I choked on a breath as his thumb found my clit.

As he fucked me with his hand.

As his cock throbbed between my ass cheeks, only inches from where I needed him.

The climax that followed didn't give me the relief I needed.

"Please," I moaned, my hips arching of their own volition, trying to pull him closer. To take what I needed.

"It kills me when you beg for me," August snarled into my ear. "You will never have to beg when heat is over. Never. You take my cock wherever and whenever you want it."

"I want it now." My hand slipped between my thighs, looking for him.

He rolled me onto my back before I could grab him, pinning my body beneath his. When I fought weakly, the fire in his eyes flared brighter.

He captured my hands and pinned them above my head. "Look what you do to me, Fireball." He sat up on his knees and fisted his cock. Drops of his pleasure dripped down to my core, and my back arched as the scent of his need mixed with my own, flooding the air.

"You like that?" He pumped his cock again, and more of his pleasure melded with mine.

I cried out, and it pushed him over the edge.

He roared, covering my clit with his desire as he lost control. His thick fingers were sliding over my hot skin again in a heartbeat, pushing the slickness of his pleasure inside me while he got me off once more.

The pain came back as soon as my lust faded away... but the scent of us lingered in the air.

It smelled better than anything else ever had.

It smelled *right*.

THE NEXT DAY, I started shivering.

Not because of the sexy times.

Because the pain was so bad I just couldn't help it.

August swore viciously as he held me in his arms, gripping me tightly and promising he would make sure I was okay. That he would do whatever he had to, to make sure I was okay.

THAT WAS how we spent the rest of heat—trapped in bed together while I suffered and August wrestled every instinct he had.

It felt like a lifetime of pain and pleasure.

But the final day eventually passed.

As if someone had flipped a switch, my agony eased suddenly, and I could breathe normally again.

The fire in my veins seemed to be seeping out quickly.

A tired glance at the window showed there was no light creeping in through the edge of the curtains.

It was probably the middle of the night.

August's hand slid slowly up my back. "Your temperature is going down."

"I'm feeling better."

"Finally." He sounded just as exhausted as I was.

Though he hadn't been feeling the same pain I dealt with, he'd been through his own personal hell.

"Did we make it?" I whispered.

"I think so." His hand continued moving over my back, though the magic forcing us together was literally disappearing as we spoke.

"Holy shit."

"Understatement."

I laughed softly.

It didn't hurt as much as I expected it to.

He continued rubbing my back.

The warmth I felt vanished completely, leaving me coated in a layer of cooling sweat.

Thankfully, my pain was vanishing along with the fire.

"I need a shower," I said, suddenly very aware of the dampness between our bare bodies.

The clothes that had been in place to keep us from sealing our bond were long gone. I didn't care where they went, either.

"I can manage that." August's voice was still gravelly.

He eased me into his arms, and carried me to the bathroom without pause.

My cheek met his chest. "I can handle it myself, if you want space."

"Space is the last thing I want right now, Fireball." His blunt answer eased my uncertainty. He set me down on my feet, and my legs shook. So, he lifted me onto the countertop and set me there. "Let me find Eli. I'll send him into town for food."

"I'm not hungry."

"You will be." He kissed my forehead lightly, but lingered for a long moment before he finally left the bathroom.

Shock set in as I stared at the empty, open doorway.

We'd done it.

We'd actually survived heat without sealing the bond.

August had been right. We'd needed to become a team, and we had.

But what came next?

Uncertainty warred in my thoughts as I waited for my dragon shifter—who wasn't mine anymore.

fourteen

ELODIE

AUGUST CAME BACK MOMENTS LATER, picking me up off the countertop and carrying me into the bathtub with him.

Neither of us mentioned clothing, or the future, as he eased us into the large tub.

It wasn't big enough, considering the man's size, but I'd take what I could get.

Especially when *what I could get* was only a little more time spent with his body against mine.

He scrubbed us both with the unscented, four-in-one body wash, then took his time with my hair, washing and conditioning it.

My chest remained against his almost the entire time, letting him make all the decisions. Maybe some women would've wanted to be in control, but in that moment, I wasn't one of them.

"You're still hard?" I whispered, my face nestled comfortably against his neck.

"You're still naked." He squeezed my ass lightly, as if emphasizing that fact.

"You're hardly a stranger to my bare body at this point."

"Is that supposed to make me want you *less*?"

My lips curved slightly.

I didn't have the energy for a full smile, or to consider what his interest may or may not mean.

"I still want you, too."

"Good." He squeezed my ass again, his touch gentler than it had been while we were under heat's influence.

I smiled against his neck.

We stayed in the tub for ages, relaxing in the water even as it cooled.

For what felt like the first time in forever, I wasn't sweating.

There was nothing pushing me to need August. Nothing pushing me to touch him.

But I still loved the feel of his body against mine, and his hands on my skin.

And I still wanted to know what it felt like to have sex with him.

One last hurrah, maybe?

He didn't seem entirely over me yet. Maybe that would come with the sunrise or something.

I wasn't about to ask him at the risk of ruining our final moments together.

Eventually, Eli knocked on the door, and we got out of the tub. I pulled on one of August's t-shirts, not bothering to put anything beneath it, and he pulled a pair of sweats up his gigantic thighs.

They hid even less than my shirt did.

His hand captured mine, and our fingers laced together as we walked through the cabin. He didn't release my hand as he opened the door, or as he grabbed the bag off the doorstep and closed it again.

We finally let go of each other when we sat down on the couch with our sides nearly connected.

August opened the bag of food, and paused when he found a note inside. I looked over his shoulder in an attempt to read it, but he crumpled it up before I had the chance.

Then, he burned it.

"What the hell?" I frowned.

"It was just Eli being Eli. Nothing to worry about."

I assumed it was a sex joke of some kind, based on that comment, but I still would've liked to see what it said. It wasn't like I couldn't handle a sex joke. My *life* had been a sex joke for four weeks.

He opened the food, and I was immediately distracted.

My stomach rumbled loudly, and he handed me a fork.

Two entire to-go containers of food followed.

And both of us fell silent as we devoured it, bite after glorious bite.

When it was gone, I was full, and even more exhausted than I'd been before.

We set our empty containers to the side, and August tugged me onto his lap. My shoulder was against his chest as I leaned into him sideways, and his arms wrapped around me loosely. It wasn't our typical position, but it was still nice.

Really nice.

Especially without any magic making me all hot and bothered.

"Want to watch a movie?" His voice was quiet, but I didn't think much of it.

"You're not tired?"

"I am. Just not ready to go to sleep yet."

"A movie works, then. But I'll probably fall asleep on you."

He turned me around so my chest faced his, and pulled me closer. My face pressed against his neck, and he inhaled slowly.

Deeply.

Like he wanted to embed my scent into his lungs.

He turned a movie on—some chick flick we'd already watched in the past few weeks—and I relaxed on his lap.

"You're beautiful." His voice was quiet. "I can't remember if I've told you that."

"Thank you."

He ran his fingers through my damp hair slowly.

Sleep started to lull me in once again, but he asked me, "Can I kiss you?"

The question caught me off guard, though not unpleasantly.

"It's been a while," I said.

"Too long."

"I was surprised you weren't running away from me an hour ago, and now you want to kiss me?" My voice was playful, but not entirely. There was some truth to the question.

"I have no desire to run from you." His fingers continued to tease my hair, but his voice wasn't anywhere near playful. It was serious. Almost solemn.

I lifted my face from his neck and studied him for a moment.

His expression was calmer than it had been when I was in pain, but that was a given.

His eyes were blue again, a gorgeous blue that anyone could get lost in. Me, in particular.

"You're beautiful, too," I finally said, setting my hand on his cheek. "You probably don't want to hear that, but it's true."

His eyes shut, and he took a deep breath in.

"When we first met, I was the one doing that."

His lips curved upward. "I remember."

"It feels like a lifetime ago."

"It does." He lifted his hand to rest over the top of mine. "I'm glad I found you, Fireball."

Found, not *met*.

Like he expected us to last.

Like we weren't about to part ways for the rest of our lives.

My throat swelled, and I lifted my mouth to his before he could catch the scent of my sadness. If he could even smell me like that anymore.

The kiss was soft, and unassuming.

Not careful—we had no reason to be careful with each other. We knew each other too well for that.

But it wasn't rough, either.

It was something between that.

Something just a little magical.

One of his hands slipped into my hair, cupping the back of my head. The other caught my chin, tilting my head into the position he wanted me.

My free hand lifted to the other side of his face, holding him in place for me too.

My body warmed, but it had nothing to do with heat's magic. And everything to do with the man beneath me.

It was a kiss goodbye, and I should've been glad that he was about to walk away from me.

Instead, I was dreading the moment when I would have to let him go.

But he wasn't in a hurry, either.

He kissed me, and kissed me, and kissed me, and I gave him just as much as I got.

When I pulled away just long enough to take a few deep breaths in, his mouth moved down my throat.

Nipping.

Teasing.

Tasting.

"I want to feel your skin on mine, Fireball." His voice was low, and I heard the words he didn't say.

One last time.

I tugged his shirt over my head, and he helped me get free of it.

His hands skimmed my body, and goosebumps erupted on my skin. His palms were hot, the fire in his veins warming me in an entirely new way.

A way I *loved*.

"Take your pants off," I breathed.

He stood long enough to kick them off, freeing his cock. It sprang up between my thighs, and finally, there were no rules.

No limits to what we could do to each other.

I rocked against him, using his length to work my clit. It felt amazing, and the way he throbbed told me he agreed.

"You're wet for me, even without the magic." His voice was gravelly again.

He wanted me, badly.

I smiled. "Always, Auggie."

He laughed—a full-bellied laugh. "Never tell Eli you call me that. He'd never let it go."

My smile widened, though I fought a small wave of sadness.

I'd never get a chance to stop myself from telling Eli that.

I didn't know if I'd ever even *see* Eli again.

"Deal," I said.

His lips recaptured mine, and it was hotter.

Rougher.

More wanting—but for once, no actual need.

He rolled me onto my back, releasing his grip on my hair to keep us balanced.

August didn't bother asking me how I wanted him.

He didn't need to check what I was comfortable with, or if there was anything I preferred.

He knew me.

He knew what I liked, and what drove me insane.

And he knew that for our first time, I'd let him take the reins, no questions asked.

He pulled his body away from mine and let his eyes burn down my figure.

"I thought you were finally going to fuck me," I teased, still a little out of breath.

"I am. Just wanted another good look at you. Maybe another taste too." He lowered his lips to my nipple, and sucked lightly before releasing it with a loud popping noise.

My hips arched. "Not tonight."

His eyes lifted to mine.

He must've seen the emotions in them. "Next time."

My throat swelled again, but I nodded.

If he wanted to play like that, to avoid the sadness of our goodbye, I wasn't going to stop him.

He adjusted his grip on my thighs, then eased the tip of his erection to my core. When he dragged it over my center, taking care to circle my clit a few times, I groaned.

He grabbed my ass with one hand, changing the angle of my hips as he thrust inside me.

There was no slow and gentle.

No caution.

No uncertainty.

For the rest of the night, I was his, and he was mine.

I took an unsteady breath in as he filled me.

He was thick, hard, and powerful.

I'd never felt that full—or that *right*.

"I think you were made for me," I managed to get out, my eyes meeting his intense gaze.

"There's no question, Fireball." He pulled out, and thrust in again.

A strangled cry escaped me.

He felt so good.

So insanely good.

I hadn't been prepared for that. Nothing could've prepared me for it.

My hips moved with his next thrust, and I met his effort with my own.

Our eyes remained locked as we moved together, our breathing hard and our bodies working like they were created to do exactly that.

It wasn't fucking.

It was making love.

He bit me while I climaxed the first time—and again the second.

With the third, he swore he was never going to let me go.

When we eventually collapsed in bed together, our bodies still intertwined, I couldn't help but feel like my life would never be the same again.

fifteen

AUGUST

SOFT RAYS of sunlight filtered in through the edges of our blackout curtains, emphasizing the gorgeous lines and curves of Elodie's body.

She'd fallen asleep a few hours ago, but I hadn't allowed myself to close my eyes.

Eli's note had made it clear that the thunder wouldn't let me have another day to make sure she recovered properly from the hell we'd made it through.

I bought you tonight. You're welcome.

That was all it had said, but it had been enough.

And now, it was time for me to walk away.

I took in a deep breath of her scent, then forced myself to get out of our bed.

Dragons didn't usually carry bags when we flew, but I didn't give a fuck about tradition anymore. I needed my female's scent with me. I wasn't going to survive leaving her otherwise.

So I grabbed her backpack, carefully emptied her school stuff onto the kitchen table, then packed it full of things that smelled like her.

Two of my shirts that she'd been wearing.

The throw blanket on the couch that should've been three times as big as it was.

A couple of her hairbands.

A few dirty pairs of the spandex shorts and tiny bras that had been tempting me for weeks.

My phone, with her number saved on it.

The individual items went into plastic bags, so the scents weren't disturbed when the thunder went through my shit. They probably wouldn't let me keep the phone, but it was worth a shot.

Quiet footsteps on the porch told me my time was up.

I stepped into our bedroom one last time and took a long look at my sleeping female.

My *mate*.

Then, I stepped back.

And made my way out of the cabin.

Every breath I took as I walked away from her hurt like hell, but I kept walking.

Because the only alternative was to make her mine, condemning her to six months in a prison she could never survive.

But my chest still ached with the knowledge that I was leaving her.

Eli was waiting on the porch.

"Ready?" There was a question in his eyes, and an apology.

He and Jasper knew as well as I did that if one of them had been in Scale Ridge like they were supposed to, I wouldn't have had to make a deal with the Villins to keep our sister safe.

And if I hadn't made a deal with the Villins, I wouldn't be headed to prison.

But there was no point in dwelling on the past.

I'd survived heat to keep my mate alive. Now, it was a question of whether or not I could make it through prison long enough to get back to her and make her mine permanently.

Eli had asked if I was ready.

Of course I wasn't.

I never would be.

But I closed the door behind me anyway. "You're going to protect her."

"Of course I am." Eli slipped his hands in his pockets, crossing the front yard with me.

"Don't let her touch any other guys."

He shot me a look that told me I knew he couldn't enforce that.

My jaw clenched.

I'd just have to prove myself better than any other bastard she might take home while I was gone. The possibility of her sharing our bed with someone else made me want to kill something—preferably whichever man she tried to take to bed—but I'd have to deal with it.

I'd win her back.

There was no alternative.

"Let's go," Gordon barked.

I didn't let myself look back at the cabin as I stripped and shifted, catching my bag in my talons before I took to the sky.

I'd be back for my Fireball, and the home we'd made ours, as soon as possible.

sixteen

ELODIE

THE BED WAS cold when I woke up.

My forehead furrowed, and my arms searched the sheets and blankets for August before I opened my eyes.

He wasn't there.

That was weird, after so many weeks of waking up together.

Was he already making breakfast?

I slipped out of bed, frowning when I couldn't find the t-shirt I'd stolen from him the night before. I could've sworn I brought it back to our room.

Maybe I'd left it on the couch.

Shrugging, I grabbed a clean shirt and headed to the kitchen. My legs shook with every step, but I figured it was because of the sex the night before.

The kitchen was empty.

I stared at it for way too long.

Way.

Too.

Long.

Finally, I turned back to the couch.

My shirt wasn't there.

Neither was August.

An awful feeling washed over me.

Though I was pretty sure I knew what had happened, I checked every room in the house, my legs still trembling.

Plus the porch.

And the single vehicle in the driveway, which belonged to me.

He was gone.

Tears welled in my eyes.

He'd left me without saying goodbye.

After talking like we'd last forever the night before.

I dashed the leaking emotions away angrily.

The bastard had ghosted me.

After I suffered through heat, and had sex with him, and we'd been a team.

Yes, he was headed for prison. And yes, I'd known we'd be over as soon as heat ended.

But I'd thought I knew him better than that.

I'd thought we were friends.

The tears fell harder and faster.

I gave up on trying to wipe them away.

I was allowed to be sad for a few minutes, while I packed my bags.

Then, I was going to be furious, whether my emotions got on board with it or not. I wasn't going to cry over the douchebag who'd left without saying goodbye.

I WAS SUCH a shaky mess that I gave up on packing after a few minutes. Instead, I threw a change of clothes and my laptop in a bag. My backpack was missing too, so my stuff went in a tote I'd gotten for free from some school-related event. The bag's zipper had been broken for as long as I could remember, and there was a big coffee stain on one side of it.

I clutched my phone in one hand and my keys in another as I walked out of the cabin without bothering to lock it. Even if I'd wanted to do so, I didn't have a key.

And the place smelled so strongly of August, there was no way I could stay. The memories I had there...

I shook my head.

I couldn't let myself think about any of that.

My mind needed to stay firmly in the present.

The present, in which I needed to get back to my old apartment. Vi and Randa hadn't rented out my room, so I should still be fine to sleep there. None of my stuff was there anymore, but I'd survive.

I was practically a professional at surviving after the last few weeks.

I finally got in my car and pulled away.

Tears were still streaming down my face, but I didn't pay them any mind. I didn't have the energy to fight them, or to muster up the anger I'd promised myself.

IT TOOK me ages to get out of the forest and back to the main part of Scale Ridge.

Though I tried to focus on what was happening in the moment, my mind kept replaying the way I'd woken up alone.

August had abandoned me.

And it hurt like hell.

When I finally stopped in my old apartment's parking lot, I stared over my steering wheel for a solid two minutes without moving. My gaze was on the building I'd called home for so long, the one my best friends still lived in.

But I felt nothing.

Nothing for the building, at least.

I wiped some more tears away, and finally shut my car off.

It was useless to dwell on what would never be.

My phone rang before I got out of the car, and I halted when I looked at the screen and found an unknown number.

My stomach clenched.

What if it was August?

That was ridiculous, though. I had August's number. The one he'd use in Scale Ridge, at least. And if he was saying goodbye from Mate Mountain, he wouldn't bother calling me. He'd just text.

And he wouldn't have had to sneak away.

Even if he was being dragged off to prison, the other dragons would've let him say goodbye to his *mate*.

Although... we hadn't sealed the bond.

I wasn't his anymore, and he wasn't mine.

I let out a slow breath through my nose.

Everything was going to be okay, somehow.

I hit the button to ignore the phone call, and slipped out of my car. My bag went over my shoulder, holding the few things I'd brought with me. My apartment key was still on the loop with my car's, so I didn't have to dig for it.

My phone rang again, and I ignored it again, without letting myself consider what might happen if I answered.

My legs were still shaking.

A text came through as soon as that call went to voicemail, and I didn't have the heart to ignore it.

I was halfway up the first flight of stairs that led up to my third-floor apartment when my feet paused as I read the message. One of my hands remained on the stair rail, just in case my shaky legs decided to give out without warning.

> **UNKNOWN**
> ANSWER YOUR PHONE, EL
>
> I'M SUPPOSED TO BE GUARDING YOU, DAMMIT

I bit my lip and wrestled with my options. I could ignore the message and move on with my life... or I could figure out who was texting me.

There really weren't many options as far as who it could be. Not many people on the planet called me *El*.

> **ME**
> Who is this?

> **UNKNOWN**
> Eli

My throat swelled.

What did he mean, he was supposed to be guarding me?

My phone rang again, and I answered it.

"Where are you?" He didn't bother with greetings or pleasantries. "I try to do a good deed by going out to buy you pastries, and this is how you pay me back? By vanishing? What the hell?"

I bit my lip, hard.

"Hello?" he demanded.

"I'm here. Just... why are you calling me? And buying me pastries? And why do you think you're supposed to be guarding me?"

Someone passed me on the stairs, giving me a weird look when they heard the *guard* thing.

I forced my feet to start moving again, carrying me up toward my old apartment. I was uncertain if my legs would actually make it up before my knees buckled, but they kept moving.

"What do you mean, why? Didn't August tell you?"

"Tell me what? I thought we were good. He made it sound like he planned to stay last night—but when I woke up this morning, he was gone."

"He didn't say goodbye?"

"No." My voice cracked a little.

I wiped a few new tears away with a trembling hand.

"Shit. Want me to kill him for you?"

"I don't think he wants anything to do with me, so there's no point in that." I finally reached the apartment and unlocked it. It was the middle of the morning, around 10 AM, so Randa would be at school and Vi would be asleep.

"That's bullshit if I've ever heard it. My brother's an asshole, but he's not a liar. If he didn't say goodbye to you, it's because he plans on coming back. The thunder took him away this morning."

"It's sweet of you to lie for him, but I'm not that delicate, Eli. I can handle the truth. The thunder might have taken him to prison, but he's not coming back for *me*."

Eli growled into the phone. "He specifically asked me to keep you away from other men, El."

"Sure he did."

"I'm serious. I'll prove it, too. Where are you?"

"Don't worry about that." I sat down on the comfortable-but-weird-smelling couch my best friends and I had gotten the day after we'd moved in. It should've felt homey, but it didn't.

It felt wrong.

Smelled awful with my dragon's sense of smell, too.

"If you don't tell me, I'll be forced to eat the rest of the donuts I bought you while I track you down."

"How are you going to track me down? And why do you assume I want donuts? I thought you brought pastries? Are donuts considered pastries?"

"I don't know, but you just survived heat without giving in. You should be hungry."

I *was*. I'd just ignored the hunger in the whirlwind of my emotions.

"I'll buy myself donuts if I want them. Go home, Eli."

"I promised my brother I'd protect you, remember? That means until he's back here to keep you safe himself, I'm going wherever you are. Starting as soon as I find you. Give me your location, or I'll figure it out myself."

"Good luck with that." I hung up the phone, dropping it on the couch beside me.

Another text lit up the screen a heartbeat after the device landed.

BRYNN

How are you feeling? Did the thunder pick August up yet?

My eyes burned.

If they had, he hadn't let me see them do so.

I erased the message from my phone's screen, then stuck it between two couch cushions so it couldn't bother me.

Grabbing a throw pillow, I curled in on myself on the other end of the couch and squeezed my eyes shut again as more tears started to fall.

I was going to be okay.

I *was* going to be okay.

I just needed some time to cry first.

So I hugged the pillow to my chest and let my tears fall.

I'D DRIFTED off for a bit when a knock sounded on the door.

Clutching my pillow tighter to my chest, I ignored it.

A moment passed, and I hoped the person had walked away.

Instead, they knocked again.

Louder.

I blinked the sleep from my dry, crusty eyes.

The person knocked *again*.

Something told me I knew who it was.

My phone started to ring in the crack between couch cushions

I ignored it without looking down at the screen.

The call went to voicemail.

A text came through a moment later. I accidentally saw the top half of it on the part of the screen that showed over the cushions.

> ELI
>
> Open the door or I'll break it down

My forehead creased.

Would Eli actually break my door down?

I considered it for a long moment before deciding he wouldn't.

Then, I sent him a middle-finger emoji.

He sent an angry one back.

> **ELI**
> I'll be forced to eat all the donuts if you leave me out here

Did I care if he ate all the donuts?

My stomach growled loudly at the thought of the sweet *pastries*.

Maybe I cared.

I stared at the door, arguing with myself for all of one minute before I finally crossed the living room and opened it. My legs shook with every step. My body felt weak, for some reason.

The gigantic, blond shifter stood on my doorstep with a donut in his hand. There was a single bite taken out of it.

I plucked it from his fingers, then grabbed the purple donut box from him and walked back to the couch.

"You look..." he started, trailing off when he realized he had nothing polite to say.

I took a vicious bite of my donut.

The chocolate glaze melded perfectly with the abundance of sugar in my mouth.

The way I looked didn't matter.

"I told August I'd give Jasper updates about you," Eli finally said. "What am I supposed to tell him?" he gestured to my face, which was probably red, blotchy, and a little swollen.

I took another violent bite.

Its deliciousness would not sway me.

"I thought of a way to prove it." Eli changed the subject again.

"To prove what?" My mouth was full when I spoke.

"That he's planning on coming back. Here." Eli tapped the screen of his phone a few times, then handed it to me.

I scanned the text conversation.

> **AUGUST**
>
> I put the cabin in her name. She should get an email a day or two after I'm gone. Tell her after heat ends, so she knows she doesn't need to leave.
>
> **ELI**
>
> Tell her yourself
>
> **AUGUST**
>
> She's dealing with enough right now
>
> **ELI**
>
> She'd rather hear it from you
>
> **AUGUST**
>
> Just tell her

The date on the conversation marked it as taking place a week and a half before heat ended.

"That doesn't prove anything. Transferring a *mortgage* to me when I don't have a job doesn't exactly seem like a kindness."

"There's no mortgage. Dragons get paid well to protect the prison. I'm sure you know that."

He *had* mentioned buying Eli a cabin when he bought his. We just hadn't really talked about money before.

I finished off my donut and grabbed another one from the box.

It was far emptier than it looked like it had started, which made me flash an annoyed look at Eli.

He lifted his hands as if in surrender. "He wanted you to have a place to live after graduation, and he thought it was yours as much as it was his."

"He wouldn't have put it in my name if he was planning on *coming back.*"

Leaving it to me was just another wordless goodbye.

"Of course he would. August didn't want you to move out while he was gone."

I scowled.

"Check your bank account," he added.

"Why would I do that?"

I knew my bank account was looking grim. I'd been aware of that before I met August. My scholarship money was about gone, and I only had a two-month cushion to start my job in Scale Ridge, or I'd need to move back home.

I'd already emailed Brynn's brother-in-law about working for his vampire-hunting company, and he'd agreed to hire me after all of the mate stuff was sorted out.

So I had a job... potentially.

One that would remind me of August constantly.

"Just do it, El."

I took another bite of my donut.

He sighed, crossing the room to sit down beside me. When he grabbed my phone off the couch, he tilted it to unlock the device with my face. Then, he went looking for my banking app.

Eli scanned my face again after pulling it up, then placed the screen in front of my eyes.

I stared at it for a long, silent moment.

And another.

And another.

Then I finally ripped it from Eli's hand, my forehead creasing as I stared.

There were more numbers than there had been the last time I opened it.

A lot more numbers.

I clicked around, finding my name at the top, then opened up my transactions to find multiple large deposits from an *A Sky*. They had been occurring throughout the past month, so I knew Eli hadn't just wired the money.

"What the hell?" I finally asked, looking at the dragon again.

"I told you, he's coming back," Eli said. "He would be here right now if he wasn't in prison."

I shook my head, dropping my phone back on the couch.

It would take me ages to process the money thing. And the cabin thing.

But ultimately, none of those proved what Eli thought they did.

"August felt bad about putting me through heat, and about the pain I felt during it. If he's as rich as you're suggesting, leaving me the cabin and a ton of money isn't a sign he's coming back. It's an apology." I put the rest of my donut down, my stomach clenching.

I was still hungry, but I was also sad.

And hurt.

Tears were stinging my eyes all over again, refusing to dry up for good.

I'd cared about him.

Maybe I'd even been falling in love with him.

And he left me without a goodbye.

"He bit you," Eli pointed out.

My forehead creased.

He gestured to the back of my neck, where August had bitten me the night before.

"His bite gives you his magic for *months*. It takes ages for the power to work its way out of a human. The scar looks fresh, so he must've just bitten you. He wouldn't have given you more of his magic if he wasn't planning on coming back. Surviving the prison would be hell at full strength—it'll be worse with part of his power embedded in your veins."

My forehead creased further.

I didn't have an argument for that.

He *had* spoken like he wasn't leaving me the night before.

"I'm not saying this happened, but if a dragon were to bite a human *twice* in one night, what would it do?" I asked.

Eli frowned. "Twice?"

"I didn't say it happened," I said quickly.

His frown deepened. "I don't know. It might give you more of his magic, or make that power remain longer. Or it might not do anything outside of pleasure. Biting is supposed to be enjoyable."

Oh, it was.

My face warmed at the reminder of the way he'd bitten me while he fucked me from behind.

His hands on my breasts.

On my ass.

On my clit.

"You reek of him," Eli said, his nose wrinkling. "Whatever you're doing to make the smell worse, stop."

I hadn't showered yet.

And I didn't know if I wanted to. Not when it would take his scent off my skin.

Was the lust in my memories making me smell *more* like him?

I lifted his shirt to my nose and inhaled.

My body relaxed immediately as I breathed in his scent.

He smelled *so* good.

Would I ever be able to let him go, even if he really had walked away for good?

seventeen

ELODIE

I FORCED myself to pick up my donut again. My hand still trembled a little.

It was my turn to change the subject. "Do you know why I feel so weak?"

"Weak?" The wrinkles on his forehead deepened. "No."

Great.

"No one survives heat without sealing the bond, remember? We're in new territory here. You two are legends at this point. Don't be surprised if a few members of the thunder show up to question you. We both know August won't answer any of their questions."

If he wouldn't, I wouldn't either.

"I'll need something to tell Vi and Randa when they get home and find me struggling to get off the couch," I said.

"What do you mean, *struggling to get off the couch*?"

"I told you, I feel weak. My legs are super shaky. They have been since I woke up. I thought I was going to crash on the stairs earlier."

"Give me a second." He grabbed his phone and tapped on the screen a few times, then lifted it to his ear. It wasn't on speaker, but my hearing had improved just a little bit with August's magic too, so I could hear it ringing clearly.

"What?" An irritated male voice answered.

I was pretty sure it was Jasper's.

"We've got a problem."

"More of a problem than having our oldest brother in prison?"

Eli glanced over at me.

I tried to act like I wasn't overhearing anything, simply taking yet another bite of my donut.

"Yeah," he finally said.

Jasper growled. "What is it?"

"Elodie feels weak."

There was a moment's pause.

"*Weak*?" Jasper asked. "What do you mean, *weak*?"

"She says her legs have been shaking ever since she woke up. She's having a hard time walking."

"Is August's magic wearing off? I figured he would've bitten her before he left."

Eli glanced at me again. "He did. Twice."

"Then she shouldn't be *weak*."

"Nope."

"It's got to have something to do with heat ending."

"That's what I was thinking. Figured I'd better get a second opinion, given we're dealing with August's mate."

"Yeah," Jasper grumbled. "Try to get to the bottom of it. If you can't get it figured out, I'll head into the prison to see if August knows anything. If I start asking questions, he'll realize something is up, so I'd rather avoid that."

"Agreed."

"Call me in a few hours."

"Will do."

They ended the call like that, leaving Eli to stare at me like I was a puzzle to solve.

I took another bite.

I was going to finish the whole box at the current rate. I'd probably still be hungry when I did, too.

"When are your friends getting back?" he asked me.

"I don't know." I hadn't been talking to them like I used to. Heat had consumed me for weeks.

Randa would be finishing up one of her last finals.

Vi would be...

Sleeping. Right.

I looked at the time.

It was nearly noon.

She'd be up soon. She slept with blackout curtains, an eye mask, and ear plugs, so I knew she hadn't heard us. Her shifts at the restaurant rarely ended before 3 AM, so she'd been forced to perfect the art of sleeping through the first chunk of the day.

"We've only got a little time to figure it out, then,"

"To figure what out?" Viola's voice was tired, but irritated. "What happened?" All she had on was a tank top and a pair of sleep shorts, so her nipples were on full display. As I expected, she didn't seem to care in the slightest.

She stepped into the living room, and her eyes widened when she saw my face.

They narrowed as she pointed them at Eli.

"The bond broke," I told her. "It didn't become permanent. Outside of the initial emotions, I feel like shit, and Eli is trying to figure out why."

Her gaze left him, and landed on me.

A heartbeat later, she was sitting beside me, hugging me fiercely.

Another round of tears surfaced, and I blinked them back as she held me tight. Neither of us said a word, but we also didn't move to let go.

"You smell amazing, Vi," Eli offered. "Just figured I'd throw that out there."

Heat obviously hadn't started between them, or he'd be acting very differently around her. He must've just been... flirting, I guess.

"Screw off," Vi tossed back, finally easing her hold on me. "What are you feeling?"

That question was directed to me.

"Really weak. Shaky. A little light-headed."

"Have you been sleeping enough?" she asked. I'd mentioned that lust played a role in the mate bond at some point, so I was sure she knew I was physically with August.

I frowned. "Probably not."

"How are you not sure?"

"The bond made things weird. It's hard to explain." I brushed a few strands of hair off my face.

She sighed. "So you're not sleeping enough. That could be part of the problem. Have you been eating enough? I have to think the big bastard knew how to feed you, at least. The man obviously eats a lot."

"He cooked a lot, I just didn't have much of an appetite for the last week or two. Couldn't choke the food down."

"And that's another bond thing?" Her expression was critical.

She knew I wasn't telling the full story.

I nodded anyway.

"So you haven't eaten enough, and you haven't slept enough. Anything else to consider?"

The sex marathons probably came into play too, but I wasn't about to spill *those* beans.

"Nope." I managed to keep a straight face, somehow.

She still didn't look like she believed me. "You most-likely just need a few days of food and sleep. If you're not feeling better after that, you should probably see whatever the dragons use as doctors."

I nodded.

I *did* feel hungry and exhausted.

Maybe a few days of food and sleep would do me good.

"You're brilliant," Eli told Vi.

She rolled her eyes. "I'll make breakfast. You can leave."

"Actually, August asked me to stay with her until he's back in town," the dragon said cheerfully. "You're stuck with me."

She made a face, then abandoned me with the shifter as she stepped into the kitchen.

I held the pillow to my chest again and let myself lay down on the couch. My eyes closed, and I drifted off, barely stirring when I felt someone take the box of donuts off the cushion beside me.

Probably Eli.

He'd want to eat the rest of them.

WHEN VI WOKE me up to eat, there was a worried crease between her eyebrows.

At her command, I tiredly filled my mouth with food before I started dozing once more.

I barely woke up when two arms slipped beneath my shoulders and led me out of the room.

"What did he do to her?" Vi whispered, her voice tight and angry.

"A potential mate bond overwhelms both halves of the couple with lust," Eli murmured back. "I don't think you need more details than that."

"She wasn't hurt?"

"Not unless she asked to be."

Vi gave an exasperated sigh. "Are you always this infuriating?"

He chuckled. "On my good days."

"I don't want to see your bad, then."

"You and me both."

The door closed behind them, and I drifted off to sleep again.

Though my body was on my mattress, my dreams took me into the sky on the back of a beautiful, silver-scaled dragon.

DAYS PASSED.

I ate, drank, and slept. When I was conscious, it was only for a few minutes. Between Vi, Randa, and Eli, there was always someone ushering me back to bed if I got up for more than the time it took to use the bathroom.

My emotions leveled out a bit as I slept, so I didn't so much as try to stay awake.

I FINALLY GOT up for good early one morning. Padding out of my room quietly, I found Eli snoring on the couch. Randa and Vi were both in their own rooms, also asleep.

A drowsy glance at the clock told me it was only four AM.

I brushed a few greasy waves from my eyes, then slipped out through the front door.

There was a balcony a few feet to the left, where I could stand and look out at the sky.

I took in a few deep breaths of air.

It smelled wrong.

Not like the forest—not like the cabin.

Not like the place I'd come to think of as home.

I lifted August's shirt to my nose and inhaled deeply.

My stomach clenched.

His scent was gone from the fabric.

I missed it.

With all that sleep and food leveling me out, I could finally think rationally again.

Eli was right. It wasn't out of character for August to leave without a goodbye if he'd decided he was coming back. And he wouldn't have left me without the cabin, and money to protect me.

And he definitely wouldn't have bitten me if he wasn't coming back for me.

But he'd bitten me.

And I mattered to him.

So he would come back for me when he could.

The front door opened again, a little louder, and Eli came staggering out. He let out a relieved breath when he saw me looking out over the balcony. "Thought I'd lost you again," he mumbled. "August would kill me."

He wouldn't, but he definitely would've been pissed.

"I'm fine," I said, turning my head back to the sky.

August would've called me out for the lie.

He would've told me we were supposed to be a team.

But he wasn't there.

My throat swelled, but no tears fell.

Eli stepped up beside me, leaning against the railing too.

"He's supposed to be in prison for *six months*?"

"That was the deal."

"The *deal*? Was there another option?" My head jerked toward him.

Eli was quiet for a moment.

A long moment.

"He had to choose between six months in prison, or leaving Mate Mountain permanently."

Ohhh.

My throat swelled more. "That's really cruel."

"I agree." Eli ran a hand through his hair. "If they'd let me or Jas do the time, we'd agree in a heartbeat. He only made that deal with the Villins because we weren't there. We were supposed to be there."

"Where were you?"

"We didn't want to leave home." There was regret in his voice. "We didn't think Brynn was in any real danger. And we were worried about exposing ourselves to more human women. We were always worried about that. He always took the risk for us, being the one to take her to dance classes, school shit, and everything else."

"It's ironic that he got stuck with me when he did, after so many years of risking it," I said quietly.

"That was fate, El. Not irony."

"Fate really screwed his life up, then."

"Nah. Jas and I did that."

A moment of silence passed.

A long, drawn-out one.

"I want to see him," I finally said. "In prison. I need to know if he's really coming back to me. I can't spend the next six months hoping if he's not."

"That's not possible." Eli didn't consider it. "The thunder would never agree to let you in, and it's too dangerous. Even if it wasn't, August would scale me like a damn fish if I took you there."

"I need to talk to him, Eli."

"I'll see if I can get the thunder to agree to a phone call." His voice told me he didn't think it was going to happen.

I didn't know much about them, but I didn't think he'd succeed either.

"I don't know what I'm supposed to do," I said, still staring out at the sky. "Six months isn't long for you guys, but it'll feel like forever to me. I'm supposed to be excited about graduating, and my new job. I'm supposed to be figuring my life out."

"He wants all of that for you."

"But I don't want it without him." My voice was frustrated, but it rang with honesty. "Not anymore. We were supposed to be a team."

"Is that what got you through heat?"

"He got us through heat." I closed my eyes, letting out a long breath. "I would've given in halfway through. The pain was *excruciating*. He's the only reason we didn't seal the bond."

"He knew you wouldn't survive prison," Eli said.

"I don't know. Probably."

"It wasn't a question, El. He knew you couldn't survive there. Not even with him to protect you. He'll be a target just because he's a dragon, but a dragon's mate inside a supernatural prison? There would be carnage. The person to end your life would be seen as a hero. You'd have to be placed in the isolation cells, and no one survives the isolation cells with their sanity intact."

"Do you think he would've sealed the bond otherwise?"

"He's the only one who can answer that, but I'd say there's a damn good chance."

We both fell quiet, staring out at the sky together.

"Do you miss flying?" he asked me, after a few more minutes.

"More than I know how to explain." My whisper was soft, but sure.

"I'm sorry," Eli said.

"Me too."

We both stood out there until the sun had risen over the horizon—then, we slipped back inside the apartment that didn't feel like home anymore.

GRADUATION WAS THAT EVENING.

Randa had picked up my cap and gown, so when she pulled me out of the apartment, I went to the university with her.

No one said a thing about the giant blond guy tailing me, so I assumed someone had filled the school in on my dragon situation.

I stood in line when I was told to, walked when I was supposed to, and listened half-heartedly to the ridiculous speeches about reaching for the stars and achieving things we'd never dared dream.

I accepted my diploma when I was supposed to, shook hands with people who smelled wrong, and hugged other students I vaguely recognized. My family hadn't come, because I hadn't updated them about our bond breaking.

That was going to be a difficult conversation. Something to worry about later, though.

When the ceremony finally ended, I was exhausted, and ready to go home.

Instead, I let Vi and Randa drag me out to a nightclub.

The twins laughed about ridiculous things that had been said during the ceremony while Viola drove, with Eli following us in August's car.

It was the first real moment of normalcy I'd had since heat started, but it didn't *feel* normal.

It felt hollow.

And I had no idea what to do about that.

eighteen

ELODIE

THE MUSIC WAS SO LOUD, I had a headache before I even stepped into the club. The barrage of smells made my stomach hurt, too.

I pasted a smile on my face, though, and followed my friends to the bar.

When Vi bought three rounds of overpriced drinks, I drank them like I wasn't shrinking inside.

Like I wasn't longing for the cabin I'd left behind.

Like I didn't miss August so much it hurt.

It was ridiculous for me to feel so attached to him. I knew it was.

But that didn't change the way I felt.

I'd spent one month with him... and that month had changed everything for me.

But I forced myself to dance.

To smile.

To laugh.

"You look good," Randa teased me, swiveling her hips while some gorgeous stranger held her close. Her eyes were bright, and her face was flushed. And despite my own emotions, I was chest-achingly glad she was having fun.

"So do you," I rolled my hips too, but halted when a pair of hands landed on my waist.

They were the wrong size.

Not big enough.

Nowhere near hot enough.

And the body that stepped up behind me definitely wasn't the one I wanted there.

"Hey," the guy called over my shoulder. "You want to dance?"

Randa gave me a thumbs-up as her date spun her away from me.

Vi was back at the bar, arguing with Eli about something. They always seemed ready to rip each other's heads off.

I was on my own.

My stomach clenched at the idea of having my body pressed against someone other than August.

But before I could say no, the guy had already started moving my hips himself, grinding my ass against him.

The feeling was so wrong, my stomach literally *flipped*.

I ripped his hands off me and rushed across the room as my belly churned.

My knees hit the cold tile, and my chin hit the icy porcelain as everything in my stomach came back up.

I vomited again, and again. The feeling of nausea remained, as if every part of me was in denial that I no longer belonged to the blond dragon I wanted.

The one I was starting to think I loved.

A few tears leaked down my cheeks as I finally sat back on my heels.

What was I doing with myself?

I was in a nightclub when I wanted to be hiding away.

I was trying to have fun for my friends' sake, when I needed to give myself time to grieve.

My shaking hand wiped across my clammy forehead.

I needed to go home.

Back to our cabin.

It would feel empty without August, but it was the closest I could get without having him there.

My body worked on auto-drive as I rinsed my face and

cleaned my mouth. As I said goodbye to my friends, and asked Eli to take me back to the apartment.

As I packed up the small bag of my things.

As I drove back to the cabin, giving Eli one of the furnished guest rooms August and I hadn't touched. I didn't love having him in our space, and he smelled wrong, just like Brynn had, but the intensity of that seemed to have faded with heat's end.

And as I collected all of the blankets and pillows that smelled like him, dragging them into my room and building a nest for myself.

When I fell asleep that night, I felt more at peace than I had since I woke up alone in our bed.

VI AND RANDA drove over the next afternoon.

They were both hungover, and confused about why I'd left.

I made pancakes and smoothies for them while I explained.

"I know it's weird, but I feel like this is where I belong."

They exchanged looks that said they thought I was crazy.

I *was* crazy.

So, there was no way around that.

"Plus, he put it in my name. It's paid off. I only have to pay for utilities," I added.

They understood that one more.

Money was simpler than fate.

"Why did he do that?" Randa asked, her expression something between perplexed and suspicious.

"Because we were a team," I said simply. "The bond didn't seal, but that doesn't erase the feelings we have for each other. When he's back in town, he'll come here."

"Then why did he leave in the first place?"

That, I couldn't explain to them.

"Dragon stuff. He would've stayed if he could," I said.

It wasn't really a lie.

"You know this is insane, right?" Vi asked. "Like, verifiably insane. Check you into a mental facility, insane."

I rolled my eyes. "I've been living here for a month. Why is it insane that I feel comfortable here? Or that I have feelings for a guy who treated me really, really well?"

"Because you're not mates. And to supernaturals, that means you're absolutely nothing. Right?" Vi looked at Eli, who was on his phone at the table, sitting behind them.

"Hmm?" He lifted his gaze absentmindedly.

He was probably playing a game or something.

"How many supernaturals are romantic with people they're not mated to?" she demanded.

"Oh. Uh, none. Not that I know of." He looked down at his phone again.

I fought the urge to throw something at him.

Something hard.

Or a pancake, since that was nearby.

Yeah, dropping a syrupy pancake on his head would be extremely satisfying.

"So he's not going to be with you," Vi pointed out.

"Could the bond restart again, Eli?" Randa asked. "Since it didn't seal last time?"

He looked up again, his forehead creasing for a moment. "I'm not sure."

That made my chest hurt a little.

"I'm going to stay long enough to figure it out," I told the girls. "If he wants to walk away from me, that's fine. But if he doesn't, I'm not leaving either."

"Being the person who cares more never works out," Vi warned.

"How do you know I'm the one who cares more?"

"August isn't *here*. You are."

"He would be here if he had the choice," I said. It was what Eli had told me—and what I desperately hoped was true.

"Elodie is old enough to make her own decisions," Randa said, reaching over to squeeze my hand. I gave her a small smile. "Let's talk about something else. Like jobs. I got a job offer a few days ago."

My eyes widened. "You did? And you didn't tell me?!"

"You were sleeping off weeks of sex!"

"Valid point. Tell me everything," I ordered.

She smiled, launching into the story about her interview and everything that had come after.

THEY STAYED for dinner before they finally headed home. Vi had work the next evening, and needed to run a few errands before she called it a night. Randa had to buy some things for her new job.

In the past, I would've probably gone with them.

In the present, I just wanted to curl up in my room, surrounded by August's scent, and read a book or watch a movie.

I took a long shower after they were gone, then padded out to grab a snack. While I was in the kitchen, I heard Eli's voice in the other room.

"How bad is he?"

How bad was *who*?

August?

I abandoned my snack idea and hurried across the house, stopping just outside Eli's door.

There was a moment of pause before he responded to whoever was on the other line.

"How many days do they think it'll take him to heal?"

My heart squeezed painfully.

Was August hurt?

"You need to get him out of there," Eli finally said. "I know the thunder doesn't want to let him go, but try to convince them."

Another moment passed.

My heart pounded erratically.

Eli growled, "If it comes down to it, I'll fly in there myself and convince him to abandon them. He's better off banned from the mountains than dead in prison. I finally have Elodie convinced he's coming back for her—I don't want to have to break the news to her that he was fucking *killed*."

I couldn't hold myself back anymore.

Pushing the door open, I stepped into the room.

Eli grimaced when he saw me.

"What happened to him?" I barely recognized my own voice.

Eli didn't answer right away.

I gave him a minute before crossing the room and taking the phone from him.

"Who is this?" Somehow, my voice didn't shake.

"Jasper," the one on the other line said. "I imagine this is Elodie?"

"Yes. Tell me what happened."

There was a moment's pause before Jasper spoke again. "August has been getting in fights. In the prison. He doesn't start them, but he finishes them. He's killed a dozen other prisoners already. The last guy to challenge him was a particularly nasty werewolf."

"And?"

"And he's in bad shape. In the infirmary. It'll be a week or so before he's fully healed."

"A *week*? Don't supernaturals heal fast?"

"Yes."

So when Jasper said *bad shape* he meant *on death's door*.

"What are the odds he won't pull through?"

Jasper was silent for a moment. "Pretty low," he finally said. "He's got someone to fight for now."

Me.

He was talking about me.

I squeezed my eyes shut. "He's not going to survive six months in there, is he?"

"It's possible, but not likely."

"And he knew that, going in?"

"Dragons run the prison, El. Everyone inside hates us. On top of that, we have to be chained so we can't shift, when we're serving time."

So August couldn't defend himself in his dragon form, even though the other prisoners probably had access to their magic.

And they would all be targeting him.

That was why he knew he couldn't let me go with him. Because it would be a miracle if he survived—but there wasn't a chance I would.

"I need to see him," I said.

"That's not possible."

"Then *make it* possible, Jasper. He shouldn't be alone while he's healing, and I'm his mate. Or *sort of* his mate. That means something, doesn't it? Even if he doesn't want me, I just spent heat with him. Maybe I can talk to the dragons and convince them to let him go earlier or something? Eli said they want to know how we made it through without sealing the bond. Can I bargain with that?"

The words were spewing from me, almost nonsensically. It didn't matter whether or not I made sense. I just wanted to see August, to make sure he was okay.

We were a team, if nothing else.

I was going to believe that until he specifically said otherwise.

"If you can convince Eli to carry you to Mate Mountain, I'll put you in front of the guys making decisions for the thunder. I can't get you in on my own," Jasper finally said.

"Thank you. I'll figure it out."

"Good luck." He hung up the phone, and I handed it to Eli.

He was already shaking his head. "August will *kill* me."

"Not if I'm standing between you two. Please, Eli? You're the one who said he won't survive on his own in there. I need to see him, to make sure he's okay, and try to talk him into coming up with another plan."

Eli sighed heavily.

"Please?" I clasped my fingers together.

"Fine." He ran a hand through his hair. "If anyone asks, I'm telling them you held a knife to my balls."

"Deal." I didn't bat an eye at the crude visual. "I'll bring a chef's knife, just to sell it."

He sighed again, but waved me toward the kitchen.

A few minutes later, I was on his back, and we were on our way to Mate Mountain.

FLYING with Eli wasn't anywhere near as peaceful as flying with August.

For one, Eli smelled bad.

For another, he didn't try to glide, or to make the ride steady. The bastard was all over the place. Up and down, zigzagging, side to side... he never flew smoothly for more than a few seconds.

It was unnerving.

I dropped my chef's knife after one particularly sharp motion, and wrapped both my arms around his stinky, scaly neck.

The last thing I needed was to plunge to my death on my way to find August.

THE SUN HAD SET and I was utterly exhausted, when we finally reached the mountain. It towered over all the others around it, and from the outside, looked pretty much like everything else.

Eli landed on a smooth, well-disguised stretch of stone, and I looked past him as he set me down on my feet.

My bare feet, I realized.

I hadn't dressed for the part. Not that I knew what part to dress for when surrounded by dragons—but I was pretty sure spandex shorts and a big t-shirt tied at my hip weren't it.

Oh well.

I could see fine in the dark thanks to August's magic, so I didn't have a problem looking curiously at the mountain.

It seemed surprisingly normal.

"This is Mate Mountain?" I asked Eli, as he shifted back while I was looking away from him.

"Yep."

I heard fabric rustling.

Hopefully he was putting pants on. I'd noticed a stone basket of something off to the side of the platform, and it seemed reasonable to assume it had clothes in it.

"It's technically called *Main* Mountain. The dragons live in the top half, and the prison is in the bottom. We corrected people at first, but realized that if they think the place we live is separate from the prison, both are safer," Eli said. "And Mate Mountain is catchier."

Huh.

That was kind of brilliant.

"Come on." He waved me into an opening in the wall of the mountain, and I followed him inside.

The interior wasn't lit. There were no lightbulbs, but they weren't necessary with a dragon's sight. My vision in the dark was fine, but the shifters' was probably much better.

There was no decorative furniture, plants, or hanging art as we moved through large hallway after large hallway.

The space was cold and impersonal, but we kept walking.

"I'm taking you to one of the gathering rooms," Eli said. "Jasper will already have the thunder together."

That was good.

I didn't want to wait. There was no point in waiting.

But, it was still going to be a little overwhelming to walk into a room full of dragon shifters who probably hated me just because of my connection to August.

I'd deal with it, though.

We walked for a few more minutes before we finally stepped into a large room. It had multiple openings in the walls, like windows, with a massive table in the middle and gigantic chairs surrounding it.

Most of the gigantic chairs were occupied by even-more-gigantic dragon shifters.

And those bastards looked *angry*.

Eli abandoned me in the doorway, crossing the room and taking a seat next to Jasper. The guys really did almost look like twins.

I forced a small smile onto my face and lifted a hand. "Hi."

Silence all but echoed through the room.

None of them looked angrier after my greeting, at least.

Socializing had never been one of my strong suits. There was a reason I'd gotten my degree in computers, not psychology. Or marketing. Or anything that required working closely with people.

"My name is Elodie. As you know, August and I survived heat without sealing our bond." My words came out awkwardly, but I went on anyway. "I know you put him in prison, and I know he's going to die if you leave him there. I overheard Eli and Jasper talking about it. And August and I aren't together—we aren't mates—but I can't leave him to die. I need to see him."

More silence resonated.

Some of their anger shifted to annoyance.

It was time to bring out the big guns.

Or the biggest guns I had, at least.

I had no idea if it would work, but I had to try anyway.

"If you let me into the prison to see him, I'll tell you how he got me through heat without sealing the bond," I said.

Suddenly, the anger and irritation was gone.

They sat up straighter.

I had their complete attention.

"You don't want to be tied down. I get it. If you let me talk to him, I'll list out exactly what happened between us and when it happened. You don't have to like him, and you don't have to like me, but we did what only one other dragon couple has managed."

More silence followed.

Long, tense silence.

Many of the guys exchanged loaded looks that I couldn't read.

Finally, they looked at Jasper.

Another moment passed before he dipped his head. "We agree to your terms."

My heart nearly stopped.

Relief rolled through me.

"You'll shower in August's room and spend the night there, in case there's any lingering possessiveness or scent sensitivity," Jasper said. "In the morning, we'll take you to him. After you're satisfied, you give us the information."

"Should you choose to withhold it for any reason, you'll end up in prison yourself," one of the other dragons added.

A few of them growled.

A couple others stiffened.

"Mates should be off-limits," one of the guys finally argued. "Our issue is with him, not her."

"She's not his mate." Another of the guys tossed a hand toward me.

He wasn't wrong.

And there was still a chance August would want nothing to do with me once he saw me.

But it was a chance I was willing to take.

Without further ado, two of the dragons I didn't know led me back through the hallways.

nineteen

ELODIE

AUGUST'S ROOM was just as bland as everything else I'd seen in Mate Mountain.

Dark sheets.

Dark blankets.

Simple, solid-looking furniture.

No decorations of any kind.

It had open-air windows, like the ones in the gathering room. I took in a deep breath, trying to catch his scent, but the fresh air had wiped it away too thoroughly.

Knowing I smelled like Eli, I slipped into the bathroom without exploring or snooping further.

Exhaustion caught up to me as I scrubbed myself clean. By the time I pulled on a shirt from August's closet, I was ready to tuck myself into bed and sleep until it was time to find my man.

My stomach growled, but I ignored it.

I didn't expect the dragons to feed me.

They didn't even want me there.

I could survive without food though. I'd eaten more than enough to feed an army since heat ended.

I was pulling the blankets up my body when a knock sounded at my door.

Though I had to bite back a sigh, I didn't hesitate to answer it. Ignoring a visitor in Mate Mountain seemed like a good way to make the dragons hate me even more.

So, I reluctantly answered the door.

When I found Eli on the other side, with a loaded plate of food in his hands, I relaxed slightly. There was another guy with him, but the other guy looked more curious than irritated, so I didn't mind.

"How are you feeling?" Eli checked, handing me the plate.

"Tired." I accepted it, pulling it into my arms and resting it against my abdomen. My stomach growled again, and his expression turned knowing. "Hungry," I admitted.

"It still doesn't seem like you've recovered."

"I'm fine."

Eli rolled his eyes.

The guy with him looked amused.

"You should be better by now, shouldn't you?" Eli asked.

"I don't know. No one gave me an instruction manual, believe it or not."

Eli snorted. "You and August are a mess."

"I've realized that."

The guy with him grinned. "What are you going to do if he agrees to leave with you?"

"I don't know, leave? We'll figure everything else out after the fact, I guess. I don't even know if he wants me. I just don't want him to die."

It was a lie.

I wanted a hell of a lot more than that.

I just didn't want to admit it to them, in case August really did turn me down.

"He brought a bag full of your stuff back with him," the new dragon said. "He's not going to turn you down."

"He did?"

I noticed the strap of a bag on Eli's shoulder, and my eyebrows lifted when I saw my school backpack. The one that had vanished when August left.

Something told me the rest of my missing things were probably in there too.

Eli handed it over, and I unzipped it.

Sure enough, clothing items and a blanket had been neatly placed in Ziploc bags and arranged in the backpack.

I put my plate of food on the ground and pulled one out, staring at the bagged tee for a little too long.

It was the one I'd worn after heat ended, when we finally made love.

"Why are they in bags?" I asked. Him and the other guy were both still watching me, clearly intrigued.

I figured they were curious. They'd never been around human women very much, other than Eli being around Brynn. And considering he'd watched her grow up, I had to imagine that made her seem less strange than a human would.

"To preserve the scent. It's a brilliant idea," the other guy said.

I would open one of the bags and investigate for myself, when I wasn't in front of the two guys.

"Thanks for this. And for the food." I gestured to the plate. "I appreciate it. See you in the morning?"

That last question was pointed at Eli.

He agreed.

"You might have weird dreams," he said, before I took both my backpack and food into August's room. "The demons' magic is supposed to affect humans when they're hungry. Don't be surprised when it hits you."

Great.

I thanked him for the warning, closed the door behind me, and locked it too.

Opening the bag, I inhaled and sighed.

It definitely smelled like us.

And like sex.

I sealed it back up again and worked my way through the plate of food before falling asleep in the blanket that smelled like me and August.

MY DREAMS WERE full of fire.

August's mouth was on my body again.

His hands were on me.

He was driving into me.

Taking me against a wall, in a shower, in the tub we'd shared after his magic faded from my veins.

It was like being in heat all over again.

When I woke up halfway through the night, I took another shower and didn't dare let myself fall asleep again.

JASPER KNOCKED on my door the next morning.

I had been lying in bed, staring at the ceiling, wondering how August was going to react when he saw me for hours.

I didn't have any other clothes to change into, so I pulled on a bra and a pair of shorts I'd found in my backpack. August's shirt went over the top, of course.

He'd lose his shit if I showed up half naked.

Unless he didn't want me anymore.

My stomach clenched.

My mind had been running through all of the ways he could tell me he didn't have feelings for me, and the many possible ways he could tell me to go to hell.

It would hurt the most if he didn't say or feel anything, though.

I hoped Eli and the other dragon were right about him still being interested in me. The way he'd brought my backpack with him told me they might be right. But that had been so soon after heat ended, logic told me his feelings could've changed or faded.

Especially while he was hurt, and inside a prison cell.

I couldn't let myself obsess about that, though.

Dragon shifters surrounded me, one on every side as I followed Jasper through the hallway and down a set of stairs.

Those stairs were followed by more stairs.

And more stairs.

And more stairs.

So many stairs that I started to wonder if maybe the shifters' size wasn't because of their magic—it was because they spent their whole lives *climbing stairs*.

I huffed and puffed my way after Jasper.

No one offered me a hand. If August *was* possessive, having their scents on my skin wouldn't work out well for any of us.

I couldn't help but hope he would care.

That he would want me.

I counted the floors and turns as we went, embedding them into my mind as much as possible. I wanted to make sure I could find my way out, in case I got stuck or left behind.

THE FURTHER DOWN WE WENT, the more I could hear sounds echoing through the hallways we passed.

Pained moans.

Rattling chains.

Angry voices.

Something hard hitting a wall rhythmically.

My arms were around my middle and my stomach was clenched painfully, when we finally stepped into a hallway.

"Don't make eye contact with anyone in the cells," Jasper said, not pausing a beat. "Don't get close to any of them, either."

I took a step closer to Jasper.

The dragons around me tightened the gaps between us.

Silence reigned as we walked through the cold stone halls. The dragons around me kept me hidden from the prisoners' sights, and hid them from me too.

A few minutes later, we slowed to a stop.

"What do you want, Jas?" August's gravelly voice made my entire body tense.

He sounded exhausted.

Worn out.

Hopeless.

"You've got a visitor."

"*What*?" August's harsh question made me bite my lip.

My mind couldn't decide whether to focus on the sexy dreams it had been hit with the night before, or the many possible ways I was about to be rejected.

Jasper finally stepped to the side, and my gaze met August's.

He was a *mess*.

His hair was damp with grease and blood, slicked away from his face.

He had two black eyes. The bruise on one was a sickly yellowish-green color, and the other was dark purple.

He was shirtless, and his torso was covered in tattered white and beige bandages. Most of which he'd already bled through.

His pants were black, and despite the dark color, obviously stiff and stained with blood.

His normally-golden skin was pale, and he was slumped over a stone bed that I wouldn't wish on my worst enemy.

My eyes widened in horror at the sight of him.

August was on his feet in a heartbeat. The scent of his blood hit my nose, and my hand flew to my mouth as he grabbed the metal bars of his cell. I noticed thick metal cuffs on his arm and ankle, and a thin one around his throat.

"What the fuck were you thinking?" His snarl was low.

Furious.

Feral.

I didn't know if he was talking to me, or to Jasper.

My chest tightened.

He *was* going to reject me.

"Get my mate out of this prison *now*." His eyes were shifting.

Heating.

Burning.

It took a moment for the words to register.

Get my mate out.

My *mate*.

He was talking to Jasper.

About me.

Calling me his mate.

The tension in my stomach eased slightly.

The guys were right.

He was still mine.

I stepped forward, and August took a breath in.

A deep breath.

Like he wanted to fill his lungs with the scent of me.

"Fireball." His voice was strained.

I stepped up to the bars of the cell and set my hands over his.

His gaze ran over my face, slowly.

Taking me in like I was the most beautiful thing he'd ever seen.

"Hey, Auggie." My voice was soft.

His eyes closed.

The expression on his face was both pain and relief. Like I was making everything harder and easier for him at the same time.

"You don't look so good," I said.

It was an understatement.

A massive understatement.

A harsh chuckle escaped him. "You still look perfect."

My chest ached. "I overheard Jasper and Eli talking. You're going to die in here if you stay."

He closed his eyes, but didn't disagree with me. Not when he looked like he did.

"Can't you isolate him or something?" I asked Jasper. "Leave him in this room alone until his time runs out?"

"Shifters don't do well alone. Most immortal beings don't. We lose our minds." Jas didn't beat around the bush, which I both appreciated and hated at the same time.

A moment of silence passed.

An idea occurred to me. An insane thought. One I couldn't speak aloud until I'd had time to really, truly consider it.

"Can you put me in there with him for a few minutes and give us some space?" I finally asked.

The four dragons who'd accompanied me looked at each other.

August didn't say a word.

His eyes were still closed. His body was still tense.

Jasper finally said, "We can't give you long."

But when he grabbed the metal door, it opened at his touch. It must've been dragon magic, because it responded immediately, and there was no visible lock.

Did that mean August could open the door himself if he wanted to?

Or that I could open it, since I had his magic in my veins after his bite?

August remained exactly where he was as I let go of his hands and slipped into the cell.

After the door closed behind me, the dragons walked away.

I waited until I couldn't hear their footsteps anymore.

Then, I quietly crossed the small cell and wrapped my arms around August's middle lightly, careful not to bump any of his injuries.

He remained still, his body trembling slightly.

"You can hug me, you know," I whispered.

"If I get my arms around you, they'll have to rip them off my body to make me let go again." His voice was still strained.

My throat swelled.

I released his middle, and he tensed.

But when I ducked under one of his arms, slipping myself between him and the cell's bars, he groaned.

His fists tightened on the metal.

He pressed his forehead to it so hard, it had to have hurt.

I wrapped my arms around him, and he shook almost violently. "Does that hurt?"

"No." He had to grind the word out.

"Do you want me to let go, or step away?"

"Never." The answer was so vehement, I pressed my head to his chest. "You smell so good, it hurts."

My body trembled slightly too. "You didn't say goodbye, August."

"If I'd looked in your eyes and seen anything but hatred, I wouldn't have managed to make myself leave." He pulled his head from the metal, and took another deep breath in as he lowered his nose to my hair.

The shaking in his body grew worse.

I tightened my hold on him as much as I dared with all those wounds.

"You called me your mate," I said.

"You *are* my mate."

"We didn't seal the bond."

"If the consequence was anything less than your death, we would've done it weeks ago. As far as I'm concerned, you're mine."

"I can't be yours if you let yourself die or lose your mind in here, Auggie."

He took in another deep breath of my scent. "I'll figure it out."

"Eli told me your only chance of getting out is to walk away from the thunder for good. You stay and die, or you leave and survive."

One of his hands slowly released the prison's bar, and his arm wrapped around my waist. He pulled me closer—and tighter.

He didn't seem to care about his wounds the way I did.

"I can't leave them any more than I could leave Brynn as a kid, Fireball. The thunder is full of assholes, but they're *my* assholes. My family. I'm relieved not to be leading them anymore, and I don't agree with everything they believe, but I won't walk away from them because of that. They're just as entitled to trust in their traditions as I am to think they're shit."

That perspective made me trust him more, as insane as that sounds.

Who didn't want that kind of loyalty from a guy? From a friend? From a *mate*?

My political views could be different from his, and he wouldn't walk away from me for it. I could screw up badly, to the extent of throwing him in prison, and he would still stay loyal.

"They could let you die in here, August."

"They could. But they won't." His second hand finally released the metal bar, and that arm went around me too. His fingers buried in my hair as he pulled me closer. Tighter.

I hugged him back hard, realizing that was what he wanted. "You're bleeding on me," I whispered.

He gave me a low, rumbly chuckle. "At least you'll smell like me."

I couldn't suppress my smile. "You're practically a caveman."

He grunted for me, and I snorted. When he laughed, I did too. Hard.

His laughter died, and I heard footsteps on the stone floor.

"Would we ever get to seal our mate bond, if you did decide to leave with me?" I asked him, my humor forgotten.

"I think fate would send us into heat again eventually," he murmured. "Could take a few days. A few months. Maybe even a few years. But it'd happen eventually. I'd hunt down a witch and force her to figure out a way to ignite it again if I had to."

"Romantic," I drawled.

"I don't give a damn about romance. I just want you." He hugged me tighter. "I'll see you in a few months."

My eyes stung. "You better not be bleeding the next time we meet."

His hand brushed my ass, squeezing lightly. "That a threat?"

"Yep. I'm very terrifying."

"Five and a half feet of pure fire."

"Keep yourself safe, Auggie." I finally started detangling myself from him as Jasper opened the cell door.

He held me tighter. "Wait there." His growl was strained again. "Don't touch her. Don't let anyone else touch her, either. Get her far away from here." There was a pause. "Who the fuck did she ride to get to the mountain?"

"Eli," I answered for Jasper. "He smelled awful, and he's terrible at flying in a straight line."

His muscles relaxed slightly. "I've been telling him that for decades."

"Centuries," Jasper corrected.

My stomach tightened.

They really had been family for more than a human lifetime.

If I *did* go along with my plan, would I ever come first for him? Could he ever choose me over them, if it came down to it? Because I could respect loyalty in a messy situation like we were in—but I could never promise my future to someone who would abandon me if his brother asked him to.

Family was important, but if I really became his mate, he would have to consider me his family too.

Could he do that?

And just as importantly, was I willing to risk everything for the insane plan I'd come up with?

I finally let go of August and peeled his arms off of me. He was reluctant, but he eventually let go.

His hands wrapped around the bars again, his bruised face in the gaps between them and his chest pressed tightly against the metal.

My shirt was wet with his blood in multiple places, and the scent of it filled the air even more strongly than it had before.

The dragons I'd come with fell into position around me, hiding me from August again before we started to move.

My mind replayed the moments we'd shared and the facts of the situation as we walked back up the stairs.

He was hurting.

And I had to decide whether or not I could live with that.

twenty
ELODIE

WHEN WE GOT BACK to the living area of the mountain, I didn't ask them to lead me back to my room. They took me to what looked like a small cafeteria, or a large kitchen and dining area.

Eli grimaced when he saw me.

"I'll grab your food. Sit down and rest," Jasper said, striding off toward the place another dragon was already filling a plate.

I crossed the room and took the seat next to Eli.

"How bad is he?" Eli asked.

"Bad." I ran a hand through a few of my waves.

There was dried blood in them, too.

"He didn't agree to leave?"

"No. He won't abandon you guys. He says you're family."

Eli's forehead wrinkled. "And you're not?"

"I don't know. He still thinks he can survive down there for six months."

Eli scoffed. "Cocky moron."

I couldn't exactly argue in the dragon's defense. Not against the moron part, at least. And he was definitely *cocky*. That much was a fact.

"What are mated dragon pairs like?" I asked him, changing the subject.

It was a question I needed answered before I could even consider my terrible plan.

"Annoyingly close. The mental bond kind of ensures that. They're rarely separated, but when they're apart, they can communicate continuously. It drives you crazy in a way you can't help but like."

"Does the thunder always come first?" I asked.

"No. Most mated dragons spend their lives in the human world, and only come back to Main Mountain when we really need them. It's been decades since we've called a mated dragon in. The only female here all of the time is the one mated to the leader of the thunder, if he's paired off."

Wow.

"So if I mated with August after all of this is over..."

"You'd probably go back to that cabin and live happily ever after."

My throat swelled again. "Are you sure he'd be willing to leave? He won't even abandon the prison to save his life."

"Leaving now would put him in exile," Jasper said, taking the seat next to mine. He set a plate down in front of me, holding on to his too. "If anything ever happened to you and he needed the thunder's assistance, tradition would require us not to answer him. He would be alone. If he makes it through his six months, he'll regain his standing with us, and be free to live his life with you without losing us."

"You're his brothers, but you'd walk away if he chose not to keep suffering in jail?" My voice was incredulous.

"It's not us he'd lose, it's everyone else." Jasper gestured around the room, which was full of dragons eating and talking. Many of them were looking at us while they did one or both of those things.

I couldn't claim to understand completely, but it did make more sense to me after their explanation.

And after everything I'd seen of August, had he ever put anyone else's safety and well-being above mine?

No.

Then again, we had been in heat...

Argh.

It wasn't an easy decision to make. Not even a little.

Another dragon shifter came over and sat down at our table, asking Eli a question about his shift at the prison. I listened to them talk while I ate, and started to get a better feel for the way the group functioned.

They were all rough and tumble guys, but they had each other. They were a family. And they were pursuing their freedom in the best way they knew how—by hiding from everyone and everything that could get in the way of it.

AFTER WE ATE, I spent a while combing my mind for everything August and I had done to avoid sealing the bond. I wrote it out in bullet points, then summarized it. I didn't write any details about the sex, because that was none of their business, but I tried to be fairly specific.

> -decided to become a team and deal with heat together
> -gave the magic everything it wanted except sealing the bond
> -touched when it urged us to touch, spent all our time together, didn't try to stay away or push ourselves.
> -gave in to the desire when it hit, as much as possible without going all the way

It really wasn't that complicated.

August holding me while I writhed in pain, without sealing the bond, was a bigger factor than anything else I wrote down. But that was his story to tell, not mine.

The dragons seemed satisfied when I handed the page over. That made me think at least one of our strategies was new to them, but I didn't ask.

Instead, I played nice, hanging out and staying quiet as the dragons did their thing. It was interesting to see the massive guys all in their element, but my mind always went back to August.

And the stupid, insane decision I'd made after I talked to his brothers.

AFTER DINNER THAT NIGHT, I retreated to August's room under the guise of going to sleep. I waited a few hours, forcing myself to stay calm and quiet, as if I was sleeping. I heard footsteps in my hallway at one point, which made me think someone was checking up on me.

But after that, it was only silence.

I gave it another few hours just to give myself the best chance of success, then packed my backpack and slipped out of the room.

My bare feet were silent on the cold stone as I padded down the hallway, finding the stairs with relative ease. There were two large pillows in my hands, and my backpack was near bursting, but I'd make it.

I forced myself to focus on counting the floors again as I walked down, and down, and down.

The sounds of the prison didn't faze me.

I didn't *let* them faze me.

When I finally reached the right floor, I let out a silent prayer that I'd counted right, and slipped down the hallway.

I passed two prisoners on my way through the mostly-empty hallway. One of them started mumbling when I passed him, but I ignored it.

August was asleep when I reached his cell.

My heart pounded so loudly I couldn't even hear the noise from the other prisoners.

My stomach was tight.

My chest was, too.

August inhaled in his sleep—and his breath caught.

He sat up groggily a moment later, his movements slow enough to tell me he was in more pain than he'd shown when I saw him earlier.

He blinked once, and again.

I stepped closer to the cell.

He rubbed his eyes, and finally rumbled, "Tell me I'm dreaming, Fireball."

"You're dreaming." I released one arm from around the pillows and carefully grabbed the cell door in the same place Jasper had.

It opened smoothly, and I didn't try to hide my relief. "You're not even locked in here, Auggie."

"The thunder can't lock me in a prison created by dragons." His eyes narrowed. "Tell me again."

"You're still dreaming." I closed the cell door behind me, listening as the strange locking mechanism refastened itself.

He inhaled. "You don't smell like me."

"I showered and changed."

"If this is a dream, you should smell like me." His growl made my body warm.

"Maybe you're dreaming about touching me." I crossed the room and set the pillows down on the small stone bed.

That thing was going to be a bitch to share.

There was another one in the other corner, but it was far enough away that I didn't think there was a chance August would let me sleep on it.

He grabbed a pillow and lifted it to his nose. "This came from my room here."

"Did it?"

I tugged my backpack off my back and started pulling out the big blanket I'd painstakingly shoved inside it. The top half stuck out the top part of the bag, but it hadn't fallen out, so it was fine.

"This is too." He grabbed the blanket, running the soft fabric between his fingers.

I didn't reply as I pulled out a clean pair of sweats for him, some manly-smelling deodorant that we'd have to share, and one toothbrush that we would also be sharing.

Not the most sanitary of options, but hey. We'd make it work.

"Fireball." He sounded angry.

"Still a dream," I offered, zipping the bag up with the toiletries in it and setting it on the ground.

Someone would have to bring me tampons when that time of the month came around, but heat had put my period off for a good long while, so I was kind of hoping it would start again soon.

Then, we could seal the bond, and I wouldn't have to deal with a period in jail.

Best of both worlds, right?

Minus the heat bit.

I'd be happy if I spent the rest of my life without experiencing heat again.

His hands caught my hips, and he eased my body to his. He turned me around as he did, so my front met his when I finally, gently, bumped into the bottom of the stone bed.

"Still dreaming," I whispered, as his narrowed eyes moved over my face.

Finally, his mouth met mine.

It was hot.

Brutal.

Lips, tongue, and teeth too.

He ripped away from me with a snarl after a moment, his hands gripping my face. "What the hell, Fireball? Who brought you here?"

"I did." I held his gaze, defiance filling mine.

I wasn't walking away, no matter what he said.

"You can't be alone in here without losing your mind. You won't leave to save your life. This is the answer." I gestured toward myself. "Me."

"You're not staying in this fucking cell with me. I fought heat for *weeks* to keep you out of here. I watched you suffer, I forced myself not to do anything, I—"

"How do you think I'll feel when you die in here?" I demanded.

He blinked.

His forehead wrinkled, just slightly.

"Did you even think about me? You said we were *mates*, August. I woke up in our bed *alone* the morning after we finally had sex. You didn't say goodbye. You abandoned me. Eli kept saying that you were coming back, that you wanted me, but you never said it yourself. I thought there was a good chance you were going to *reject me* up until you called me your mate this morning. I thought I was coming here for nothing, because you didn't want me. I—"

His lips crashed into mine again, harder than before.

More desperate.

I tasted his blood in my mouth as the kiss opened up one of his wounds, but he didn't stop.

So I didn't either.

He pulled me closer.

Kissed me harder.

Lifted me onto his lap and recaptured my face while I sat on his erection. How he was hard with all those wounds, I didn't know.

His eyes met mine, fierce and emotional and still furious.

"I wanted you. I always wanted you, and I always will." He kissed me again roughly, but pulled away a breath later. "I'm fucking *pissed* that you followed me here. It kills me that you put yourself in danger. That you snuck into the prison. That you flew with my *brother*. But I'm enough of a bastard that despite my anger, I'm *relieved*." He brushed his thumb over my cheekbone. "Relieved that you're here with me, so I'm not alone. That we're still a team."

I bit my lip.

"I'm sorry. I should've said goodbye. I should've thought about how much that would hurt you. I should've made sure you knew damn well that I belong to you as much as you belong to me—and that I would come back to you no matter what it took. Even if it meant abandoning the thunder."

"You just told me you weren't willing to leave them."

The intensity in his gaze relaxed a bit. "I told you they wouldn't let me die, and they won't. When it comes down to it, they'll get me out. They're pissed at me, but they don't want me dead. If they did, my brothers would get involved."

My forehead wrinkled. "So they're *not* going to leave you to lose your mind or suffer?"

"Oh, they want me to suffer. To lose my mind a bit, too. They just won't let it kill me."

Ah.

Great friends and family. Really, really great.

I couldn't even pretend to understand the way dragons worked, but he didn't seem bothered about it, so I didn't say anything.

"Well, I'm not leaving," I finally said. "Not until we've had a better conversation than this, at least." I gestured between us. "Say you survive this for six months, what do we do next? What's your plan? To become Jasper's right-hand man or something?"

"I hope not to be involved in the thunder's politics at all after this. Walking away from them would mean exile, which is why I can't do it. If I'm exiled, I'm alone. If something happened to Brynn, my brothers, or you, I'd have no one to turn to. As much as I don't like it, I need them to fall back on."

Well, I liked that answer.

"I planned on going back to Scale Ridge," he said. "Back to the cabin. I figured I'd have to chase some human male out of our house and woo you again. That we could live there, unless you needed to move for work. I plan to help the Villins with keeping the vampires in check, too."

"Woo me *again*? I don't remember being wooed the first time. You just told me we were a team, and I fell for it. What makes you think you could chase off some guy who actually *tried* to romance me?"

His lips split in a grin, flashing me a look at the wound I'd tasted when we kissed. It wasn't as bad as it could've been, but it didn't look good. "I have a really big..." I lifted my eyebrows, and he finished, "Teeth."

"*A* really big teeth?" I drawled. "That's not even almost grammatically correct, Auggie."

He laughed, rocking me against his erection a little. "I'd hope your memory is good enough that I don't need to translate."

It definitely was.

"If you ever vanish after we have sex again, I'm walking away for good," I warned, gesturing to one of the walls as if that was the way I'd walk when I tried to leave. It wasn't, but the dramatic effect was the same.

"Lesson learned. Won't happen again."

"Glad we have that figured out."

He made a noise of agreement. "You do have to leave, though, Fireball. As much as I appreciate you sneaking down here half-naked with pillows and a blanket, I can't let you stay. It's not safe."

"You said that if I was your mate, I'd have to go to prison with you to keep you sane."

His eyes narrowed as he put together where I was going with that.

"Today, you said I'm your mate. Was it a lie?"

They narrowed further.

I had him by the balls, and he knew it.

"Of course it wasn't," he finally said.

"Then I have to stay with you. You'll just have to deal with it."

"Fireball..."

"Are we already back to this? I thought we established that you'd rather have me stuck in this cell with you than back home flirting up a storm at every nightclub I can find with Randa and Vi."

His grip on my ass tightened painfully, and he growled, "Graduation. I missed it. Did you walk?"

"Yep. Randa didn't give me an option."

"Good. I want to see pictures."

"I can pull them up on my phone later. We were talking."

"Right. You went partying afterward?"

"Not necessarily *partying*, but yes. They dragged me and Eli to a nightclub."

"And?"

"And what?"

"And did you go home with someone?" He had to grit the words out.

If he was having that hard of a time even asking me, he'd lose his mind altogether if he'd actually gotten out of prison and found me with someone else.

"No. I danced with a random guy, though. He grabbed me when I was on the dance floor."

August's hands tightened on my ass so much, it almost hurt. "I've never danced with you."

"You never wooed me," I reminded him. "We just became a team."

A team with really good sex.

I couldn't actually say I minded the lack of romance, when the outcome was what it was.

"Will the sex be as good between us now as it was before?" I asked. "Did heat make it better?"

"Heat made us want it more, but it didn't make it *better*. If I fucked you in here, you'd enjoy it just as much." He glanced down at the stone bed. "*Almost* as much. Because of the situation, not heat. Where did he touch you? How long did you dance?"

"Careful there, Auggie. You're starting to sound jealous."

His eyes flashed. "I *am* jealous. I'd have killed to be with you in that club."

I liked his honesty, and his confidence.

Hell, I liked pretty much everything about him. The things I didn't like were so minimal they didn't matter.

"Now answer my questions, Fireball." He squeezed my ass again.

"It was only for a second. He grabbed me, and grinded up against me. I pushed him away. His touch felt wrong, and made me nauseous. I puked in the bathroom afterward," I admitted. "Eli and my friends don't know that part. Don't tell anyone."

"I won't." His hands slid up my back, over my arms, and into my hair. "Do you hate me for being glad he made you vomit?"

I rolled my eyes. "I'd be surprised if you didn't. Maybe even disappointed."

He chuckled. "I like you."

"I like you too."

When he pulled me against his chest, I tucked my head against his neck. "I don't care how angry you are, I'm not leaving."

His chest rumbled. "I won't let anyone hurt you."

"I know you won't. We'll tell them to leave us in their shitty infirmary until our time is up."

He squeezed me tightly. "I'm a lucky bastard."

"I know you are."

He laughed again. "How much did you have to eat the day after heat ended to feel normal again."

"Oh, it was a lot more than the day after heat ended." I launched into an explanation about my long recovery that made August mad—but his anger made him hold me tighter.

He could be angry for ages if he decided to, because I was exactly where I wanted to be.

twenty-one
AUGUST

ELODIE EVENTUALLY FELL asleep in my arms. My wounds were pissed about the way I'd set us up on the stone bed with her on top of me, but letting her sleep on a rock was out of the question.

My fingers slid through her hair.

Having her there was surreal.

My time away from her had been torture—but I'd finally found relief.

She smelled amazing.

Felt even better.

And hearing her call herself mine?

It was the icing on the cake.

I was never leaving her side again. The thunder would have to get over it.

And my brothers would have to bring us more shit, because I wasn't letting her go hungry because of me.

I was never going to watch her suffer again, the way I'd had to while she was in heat.

It took a long while to doze off given the pain and discomfort of my situation. But, eventually, I drifted off with her against my chest.

ELODIE'S soft moan dragged me out of sleep.

I wrestled my eyes open, my grip on her ass tightening when she rocked her hips, dragging her core against me.

The scent of her desire was thick in the air.

I breathed it in deeply.

The smell had hardened my cock long before it woke me, and it felt fucking amazing when she rocked her hips more.

Moaned again.

One of my hands slid up to her hair, gripping the soft strands. The other remained on her backside, pulling her harder against me.

Her breathing was quick.

Her body was flushed, and sweating.

And the smell of her need only thickened.

She rocked against me harder, one of her hands curling over one of my wounds.

I grimaced at the pain of it. "Careful, Fireball."

Elodie didn't respond.

Her fingertips dug in deeper, and I winced. "Fireball?"

Still no response.

I lifted my head and pulled her hair to the side.

My forehead creased when I realized the problem.

She was *sleeping*.

She'd never had a wet dream before. Not even in the worst part of heat.

Something was going on.

"Wake up, Fireball." I raised my voice as I tugged her hair lightly, catching her hip and moving her a little.

She cried out, her back arching as she moved against me.

"Elodie," I growled, tugging and shaking a little harder. "Wake up and I'll give you what you need. Let me see your eyes."

"August," she moaned. "I need you."

"I'm here." I tugged again.

Shook her again.

She just moaned again.

Something had to have a grip on her. She couldn't wake up.

A thought occurred to me—and made me snarl.

There were demons in the prison.

Hungry demons affected humans' dreams. I wasn't sure how, but I knew they did. Long ago, there had been rules against bringing humans to the mountain because of it. After they were mated, the demons' magic couldn't touch them, but Elodie and I hadn't sealed the bond.

She was at their mercy.

And apparently, they turned her on.

She was moaning *my* name, though. She knew she was mine even under their magic's sway.

I couldn't wake her up.

But... I could give her what she needed, and hope it snapped her out of it.

My cock throbbed against her, and she cried out.

I wouldn't let myself take her. Not when she was asleep. She wouldn't have a problem with it—we'd discussed touching each other while we were sleeping during heat, and we'd both agreed enthusiastically.

But we'd only been together physically that one night. The second time I took her wouldn't be while she slept.

The cells around mine were all empty, so there was plenty of privacy when I slipped my hand into her shorts.

My chest rumbled of its own volition when my fingers slid over her soft, slick center.

She was drenched.

She cried out, grabbing my arm and holding it between her thighs so I couldn't stop touching her.

My cock throbbed, and I dragged my thumb over her clit slowly.

Lightly.

Exactly the way she liked it when we were starting out.

But it had been too long for her, too. She was sensitive. She arched against my fingers, demanding more.

I gave her what she wanted, circling her clit harder, not faster.

She finally lost control, crying out as she moved against my fingers. Her pleasure soaked my hand, making me mutter a curse as my cock throbbed harder.

She was so fucking delicious.

I wanted my mouth on her, but I held back, waiting to see how she'd react to the pleasure.

She was still holding my hand between her thighs, and I left my fingers against her clit lightly, the way I knew she'd want me to.

Her hips stopped jerking as she came down from the high, and she opened dazed eyes.

I watched her closely as reality finally began to set in. "Are you with me, Fireball?"

"I think so." Her voice was soft.

Breathless.

"I was having those damn dreams again."

"*Again?*" I growled the word.

If she'd dreamed of anyone other than me... I'd fucking kill the demons.

"Last night, I had them in your room upstairs. Eli said demonic magic can cause weird dreams. He didn't tell me they'd drive me mad with need. I barely slept," she admitted.

"Who did you dream of?"

She rolled her eyes. "You, obviously."

The jealousy in my chest settled slightly. "Did you touch yourself?"

She shook her head. "I probably should've. Maybe then I could've gone back to sleep instead of obsessing about you rejecting me."

"I would never." I pressed on her clit lightly, in punishment for her thought that I would. Her hips arched a little.

"Thanks for waking me up. And touching me."

"Don't thank me. It took everything I had not to fuck you senseless."

Her lips curved upward. "Sounds like fun. Why didn't you?"

My cock throbbed.

I was going to come in my fucking pants if she kept looking at me like that.

"You were sleeping."

"That never stopped you from eating me out."

It hadn't.

And I wanted to do it again. Badly.

She pressed her leg against my cock, lightly. The pressure was enough to make me clench my jaw against the need to fill her. My body ached from my injuries, but I wanted her more than I cared about the pain.

"Figured I should check in first since we only spent the one night together that way," I gritted out.

"I appreciate that." She pressed her leg against me harder, and I swore. Her lips curved. "I'm killing you, aren't I?"

"You have no idea."

She smiled, and pulled my cock free. Her hand wrapped around me, and I squeezed my eyes shut as I fought the pleasure.

"Have you touched yourself?" she asked.

"Tried. Couldn't get off without you. Knew you could be with someone else." The response was hard to get out with her fingers on me, and the scent of her need so thick in the air.

"Give me your fingers."

Her command nearly made me lose it.

I pushed three fingers inside her, the way she liked it. Her breath caught, and her hips arched a little.

"How do I feel?"

"Soaked." My voice strained.

"Only for you, Auggie."

The words about sent me over the edge.

"You're too close. Don't finish until you're inside me." Her command had me throbbing hard.

"You want my cock?"

"Always."

She drove me insane in the best way.

"I don't have the control to drag it out," I said, pulling her shorts to the side. "Or the patience to strip you down."

"Good. Fuck me already."

I didn't waste any more time, tugging her leg higher as I filled her.

Took her.

Made her mine.

She gasped, her breath unsteady and her eyes widening. "Forgot how big you are."

"Forgot how tight you are," I growled, thrusting into her again.

And again.

And again.

Her cries filled the air as I snarled with my release, flooding her channel with my pleasure. She tightened around me as she came with me, intensifying the feeling for both of us.

"Don't stop," she moaned, as her climax faded.

"Wasn't planning on it, Fireball." My lips brushed hers, her forehead, her collarbone, before I thrust into her again, and we were both lost to the pleasure.

IT WAS the middle of the next day when my brothers finally realized my female was missing.

As much as it pissed me off that they didn't notice her absence, I was glad to have the time alone with her. After Elodie realized I was bleeding again, she refused to have any more sex until I'd healed. So, there was nothing to do but talk.

It was nice to have time to catch up on everything we'd missed. She made me tell her about every one of my fights, and I made her tell me about every meal she could remember eating.

She needed more food.

It irritated me that I couldn't get it for her.

I heard their footsteps before I saw any of them.

"Here we go," she muttered.

I chuckled.

They weren't going to take her from me. It wasn't even a possibility.

Jasper led the group of dragons. He didn't look angry, and neither did any of the others.

"Why am I not surprised?" Eli drawled.

"Probably because I forced you to bring me here in the first place." Elodie's voice was upbeat.

Despite our location, she was happy.

I was too, though I'd have been happier if I had enough food to feed her properly.

"I'd think that should at least earn me a text or something before you disappear into the prison, El."

"You knew he was getting beat up in here and didn't tell me."

Eli grimaced, but didn't argue.

"I wasn't *getting beat up*," I grumbled. "I was giving beatings, and taking a few injuries as I did."

"*A few injuries?* Your entire body is one big wound!"

"Not my *entire* body." I nipped at her neck, and a sputtered laugh escaped her.

Jasper sighed, running a hand over his face. He looked exhausted. I felt bad that he was having to deal with the pressure of running the thunder, even though I was glad it wasn't August's job anymore. "What are we going to do with you?"

"I'll make a deal," I said, tucking my female's head under my chin. I didn't like that all of the guys were looking at her, even though she was mostly dressed, and in my arms. "If you shorten my sentence so I can take my female home, I'll give you my side of her story. I'll teach you how to avoid sealing the bond."

The guys exchanged looks.

They had wanted Elodie's story badly, but hers was only half. Hell, it was less than half. I was the reason we hadn't sealed the bond. I was the one who had to stand by and watch her suffer, hour after hour and day after day.

If they truly wanted to avoid sealing their own bonds when heat finally caught up to them, they needed to know what I knew.

"We'll discuss it," Jasper finally said. "I'll make sure someone brings food down while we do. And a proper bed. Maybe some chairs, too."

I dipped my head.

The bastards didn't care about me, but they had to care about themselves.

They left again, and Elodie leaned against me.

I adjusted my grip on her, not even considering letting go.

"You're the one who needs consistent food and water," she

said. "Look at yourself. It'll be my turn to baby *you* if they actually let us out of here."

I chuckled. "My wounds will heal, Fireball."

"Especially if I put clean bandages on them."

"It would help more if you put your *mouth* on them."

She laughed, hard.

I pulled her closer, silently thanking fate that she'd chased me to prison.

twenty-two

ELODIE

THE THUNDER DIDN'T DEBATE for long.

Rather than bringing us food, they came to retrieve us.

As we climbed the stairs, our pillows and blanket were in August's arm and hanging over his shoulder, despite my attempt to convince him that I could carry something since he was the wounded one. He even had the backpack.

He just captured my hand, lacing his fingers through mine.

When we made it up to the living area of the mountain, we ate together. Then, August left me in his room while he gave the other dragons his side of the story.

I took a long shower, scrubbing his blood off my skin and out of my hair. The only shampoo in there was more of the unscented four-in-one stuff, but I didn't mind.

We'd be back to the cabin soon enough.

August stepped into the bathroom as I started to turn the water off. His eyes moved slowly over my figure through the clear glass of the shower's door. After a moment, he finally stripped.

He didn't bother trying to get the bandages off before joining me under the water.

I smiled as he grabbed my hips and pulled me to his chest. His skin felt amazing against mine, and I wrapped my arms around his back as he held me close.

"I don't think wearing bandages in the shower is sanitary," I said against him.

He chuckled, running his hands down my back. "I don't care. They'll be a pain in the ass to get off."

"I'll undo them for you."

He didn't let go of me, though.

I rolled my eyes at him, and his lips curved upward.

He kissed my forehead, and my shoulder.

Then, he finally let go of me.

It took me a few minutes to get him completely unwrapped, and my stomach clenched more with each one I exposed.

They were *bad*.

"Who looked at these in the prison?"

"One of the other guys." He reached for his crappy soap, but I grabbed his wrist to stop him.

"You can't just throw that stuff on injuries like this, August."

"Why not?"

I blinked.

I had absolutely zero medical training, so it wasn't like I had a good answer for him.

"You just can't," I finally said.

He lifted an eyebrow at me.

I narrowed mine at him.

"Alright," he finally agreed.

But as soon as I let go of his wrist, he pumped some of the soap into his hand and started washing his torso with it.

"August!"

He laughed. "It's fine, Fireball. I'm fine."

"We shouldn't have been having sex when you look like this." I gestured to a particularly awful wound.

"Like I said, I'm fine. We're not keeping our hands to ourselves just because I'm bleeding a little."

"You're not bleeding *a little*. You're bleeding *a lot*. And your brothers don't think you're fine. Eli said you were on death's door."

August continued washing himself.

I huffed at him.

"If I die, you're going to end up with some other bastard," August said. "So I'm not going to die. There's no reason to talk about it. You're mine."

I scowled. "This is not how this is going to go, August." I gestured between us. "We're a team, remember? If I don't get to lie about being fine, you don't either."

He let out a long breath, but finally dipped his head. "My body hurts. It's going to be a few days before I'm completely back to normal. Maybe a week."

I stared at him, my eyes narrow.

"Two at the most," he said reluctantly. "We don't need to stop having sex. I don't want that. Having you here with me, treating me normally, makes me feel a lot less helpless."

I could accept that as the truth. "So you're going to let me take care of you?"

"I guess."

The reluctance in his voice almost made me snort.

"If the demons are giving you sex dreams, we'll need to head home as soon as possible. I don't want you making backward progress on recovering from heat. And I don't want their magic touching you."

"We can leave as soon as you're healed enough to fly."

He growled, but I stared him down, and he eventually jerked his head.

It seemed like a reasonable agreement to me.

He pulled me back into his arms, and I closed my eyes as I hugged him again.

It felt good to be back with him. Even without heat's magic, we were still a team. And that made me feel better about everything.

EVENTUALLY, we got out of the shower. August refused to let anyone more experienced than me touch his wounds, so I slathered him in antibiotic ointment that he grumbled he didn't need. Then, I wrapped him up in bandages, following his instructions while attempting to make them look as nice as the ones he'd bled through in the prison.

They didn't look anywhere near that good.

But the wounds were covered, and August wasn't going to let me do anything else, so I forced myself to be satisfied with it.

After we were dressed, we headed back to the food. We stuffed our faces, then called it a night, and crashed in bed together.

Though I was exhausted, I grabbed my phone and buried my nose in a book on Kindle instead of letting myself sleep.

When the sex dreams started, I'd inevitably wake up August. He needed the rest much more than I did, so that wasn't an option.

The book would keep me awake and distracted for a little while, at least.

So he slept, and I read.

TWO DAYS LATER, I was reluctantly climbing on August's back to fly home.

I was excited to go back to the cabin, but he wasn't anywhere near completely healed.

He just refused to stay at Mate Mountain any longer when I wasn't sleeping. And *not sleeping* had become an impossibility. I kept drifting off and waking up with his face between my thighs.

Which was fun—but he needed to stop opening his wounds.

So, we were headed back home.

THE FLIGHT WAS LONG, and relaxing. I fell asleep on August's back, but he flew steadily enough that I didn't fall.

We made it to the cabin soon enough, and August carried my exhausted ass right to our bed before we both crashed.

AUGUST WAS SPRAWLED over the top of me when I woke up. He'd pushed the bottom hem of my shirt up to my neck and was snoring quietly, his face resting against my bare breasts. One of his hands was tangled in my hair. The other was under my pillow.

I ran my fingers through his hair slowly.

Almost reverently.

He was gorgeous.

And he was *mine*.

It was insane. Absolutely insane.

But nothing had ever felt so right.

He kept snoring. One of his black eyes was gone, and the other was on its way to being healed too. The deepest wounds were still in bad shape, but most of the smaller ones were either completely better, or almost there.

He was recovering.

That was what mattered.

I slowly eased my way out from beneath him, replacing my body with a pillow as I did so. After I was free, I stopped in the bathroom, then headed to the kitchen. Though I was still wearing just a pair of his boxers and one of his shirts, I was used to wearing his clothes at that point. There was no need to change.

Turning quiet music on, I set my phone up next to the sink and started making pancakes. It was late afternoon on whatever day we were currently living—I didn't bother looking at the calendar—but breakfast food sounded good.

Bacon, eggs, and homemade buttermilk syrup went with the pancakes, so I whipped it all up before bringing both plates to our room.

August was still sleeping peacefully, but he needed to eat if he was going to keep healing.

I woke him with a hand on his shoulder. He captured it and kissed my fingertips, then my knuckles.

When he sucked one of of my fingers into his mouth, I laughed.

He gave me a lazy smile as his gaze moved down my figure. "Good morning, Fireball."

"Good *afternoon*, Auggie." My voice was playful.

His eyes landed on the food I was holding, and his stomach rumbled.

When I grinned, he chuckled, accepting the plate I offered. "Thanks for cooking."

"Any time." I sat down beside him on bed, and we ate together.

It was perfect.

AFTER A FEW MORE DAYS OF resting and recuperating, August was finally healed enough that we headed into Scale Ridge to talk to the Villins about our jobs.

His thunder wouldn't let him have anything to do with the jail if he worked with them, but they wouldn't imprison him

for it without a sentence from the supernatural govern-
ment, so he didn't care.

We spent the morning having informal interviews with the
Villin brothers, all three of which August knew well. At
lunch time, we ended up at Brynn's house, catching her up
on everything that had gone down. The dragons hadn't
sworn me to secrecy with witch magic yet, so I told her
everything August was comfortable with me sharing.

Some things were still taboo, though.

We met up with Vi and Randa for dinner at Vi's restaurant,
and had a good time chatting. They got to know August a
bit, and when we finally made it out, both of them admitted
they liked him.

I knew they would, though.

How could they not?

When we went home and watched a movie, curled up
together on our couch, I decided I would be insanely happy
if the rest of my life went like that day had.

...Even if I was quietly a little worried that we hadn't had
the chance to seal our bond. A tiny part of me was afraid
August was going to send some other woman into heat
every time we were out in public.

I tried to ignore that part of me, though.

THE DAYS that followed passed in a blur of job training
and mundane bliss.

August and I cooked together.

Talked.

Laughed.

Made love.

We spent our mornings sitting on our porch swing, with his arm around me and my hand on his thigh, watching the sun rise.

It was one of my favorite parts of every day.

Two weeks went by quickly. The sun was rising and we were swinging slowly, in exactly that position, when his fingers slipped beneath the t-shirt I had on and brushed my bare hip.

I sucked in a breath at the familiar sting of pain.

And the fire that raced through my veins.

August went statue-still.

Instead of confusion or terror, I felt joy.

Fierce, intense joy.

"It's starting again," I whispered.

August's grip on my hip tightened, but he didn't say a word.

Warmth rolled through my veins, along with a heady dose of desire.

I wanted him.

Needed him.

And a look at the fire in his eyes told me he felt exactly the same way.

So I lifted myself onto his lap, turning around as I did. Straddling him.

His hands slid down to my ass and pulled me closer, so I was positioned against his erection. "I can't fight it again, Fireball."

"I don't want you to fight it." I leaned in closer.

He did the same.

His lips caught mine, and he kissed me.

Slowly.

Sweetly.

As the warmth in my veins increased, the kiss heated too, until his bare body was against mine and I was sinking down over his cock.

We moved together until we both had to end the kiss so we could breathe.

He tilted my hips, changing the angle slightly, and it sent me over the edge.

My cry melded with his roar as we climaxed together, and I felt something bigger well up inside me.

Something stronger.

Something far more intense.

My back arched, and the orgasm went on, and on.

When it finally faded, we were both still struggling for breath, but I felt *different*.

More whole, somehow.

"Can you feel our bond?" August's voice was in my mind. I *felt* him there, as much as I heard him. Maybe even more.

The feeling was so intimate, I struggled to wrap my mind around it.

"Yes," I admitted, trying to reach out to him the way he had reached out to me.

His chest rumbled with something.

Joy.

Pride.

Pleasure.

"All of the above," he said.

My lips curved upward, and he captured my mouth again.

The kiss was rough, just the way I liked it.

"I love you, Fireball." Though he didn't release my lips, his voice was strong in my mind. Confident, too. He knew exactly what he felt for me.

And I knew exactly how I felt about him too. *"I love you too,"* I admitted. *"I have for a while."*

"Let's make it forever."

My mouth stretched in a smile against his. *"Forever sounds good to me."*

I'd fallen for a dragon...

And I wouldn't go back even if I could.

epilogue
AUGUST

I SWEPT my mate across the dance floor. Her silky white dress flowed with every step, but my hold on the back of the billowing fabric remained steady. The woman was going to trip if I let it go, and the last thing I wanted was an injured wife.

Especially when we were about to go on our honeymoon.

Two weeks in paradise with my female would be a dream.

"What do you want to do first when we get to the beach house?" she asked me mentally, her voice playful.

She'd been smiling all day.

Hell, she'd been smiling all *year*. We both had. Having the bond sealed steadied us both in ways we hadn't realized we needed.

"Get you in one of those little bikinis." I brushed my hand over her ass.

She laughed. *"Sounds like fun. I think we'll go through heat again in a few days."*

Our heats were short, since we'd bonded. Only two days or so, but we enjoyed every damn minute of them.

There was no more suffering.

No more desperation.

Just pure pleasure.

And fun; my Fireball made everything fun.

My eyes caught on a couple in the corner of the room, and interest held my gaze there as we continued moving. Elodie made me practice so much before the ceremony, I could do the dance in my sleep.

With her in my arms, I'd enjoy it, too.

She followed my attention, and laughed again, softly, when she saw what I saw.

Jasper sitting in the corner, his arms folded and his expression stony.

Miranda sitting next to him, chatting, with a flirty smile on her face.

"She really wants to be mated to a dragon." There was humor in Elodie's voice. "Can you imagine how disappointed she'd be if a bond actually ignited, and she realized how much her mate didn't want to be tied down? And then to suffer through heat..."

I chuckled. "Jas won't even look at her. No way in hell is heat going to ignite between them."

"Let's hope not." She leaned into my arms. "How long do you think we have to stay here?"

"Your mom stopped crying, so I think we're good to sneak out whenever."

Elodie flashed me a mischievous smile, then caught my hand and tugged me through the crowd.

Someone called out behind us, but we were already gone.

We were a team, after all.

afterthoughts

This book is the first time I've ever written three series set in the same world.

Weird, right?

I realized around when I started it, that I usually get bored and move on after the second series.

facepalm

Can someone please send me a better attention span?

Thanks in advance ;)

Surprisingly, instead of my typical boredom, I had an absolute blast with this book. Did I at times want to write something absolutely different and completely left-field?

Yes, yes I did. Alien romance, anyone? No?

But I think I'm sticking with these fun PNRs for a bit (knock on wood). I LOVED August and his Fireball. They made me smile, laugh, and feel all the things, and I hope they did for you too. I'm really excited to write Randa's story, and get a little more information about Mate Mountain on the way.

Her book will be called *Never Flirt with a Dragon*.

Aren't the Sky brothers fun?

I think they're fun. Don't tell me if you don't!

Anyway, I can't wait to see what happens next! If you haven't read Brynn's story yet, and you're interested, it's the third book in my *Deceit & Devotion* series.

As always, thank you so much for reading!

All the love,

Lola Glass <3

stay in touch

If you want to receive Lola's newsletter for new releases (no spam!) use this link:

LINK

Or find her on:
FACEBOOK
TIKTOK
INSTAGRAM
PINTEREST
GOODREADS

all series by lola glass

Check out Lola's website for a guide to which of her series are connected!

https://www.authorlolaglass.com/where-do-i-start

Standalones:

Mate Mountain

Wildwood

Deceit & Devotion

Claimed by the Wolf

Forbidden Mates

Wild Hunt

Kings of Disaster

Night's Curse

Outcast Pack

Feral Pack

Mate Hunt

Series:

Burning Kingdom

Sacrificed to the Fae King

Shifter Queen

Wolfsbane

Shifter City

Supernatural Underworld

Moon of the Monsters

Rejected Mate Refuge

about the author

Lola is a book-lover with a *slight* romance obsession and a passion for love—real love. Not the flowers-and-chocolates kind of love, but the kind where two people build a relationship strong enough to last. That's the kind of relationship she loves to read about, and the kind she tries to portray in her books.

Even though they're fun stories about sassy women and huge, growly magical men ;)

9 798869 364432